LOVING LUCY

LOVING LUCY

•

Noelene Jenkinson

AVALON BOOKS
NEW YORK

Jen

Published by Thomas Bouregy & Co., Inc.
160 Madison Avenue, New York, NY 10016

Library of Congress Cataloging-in-Publication Data

Jenkinson, Noelene.
  Loving Lucy / Noelene Jenkinson.
      p. cm.
  ISBN 978-0-8034-7773-5 (acid-free paper)   1. Child
care workers—Fiction.   2. Self-realization in women—
Fiction.   3. Motherhood—Fiction.   4. Australia—Fiction.
5. Indonesia—Fiction.   I. Title.
  PR9619.4.J46L68 2010
  823'.92—dc22

                                                    2010005511

PRINTED IN THE UNITED STATES OF AMERICA
ON ACID-FREE PAPER
BY HADDON CRAFTSMEN, BLOOMSBURG, PENNSYLVANIA

Chapter One

Lucy McCarthy stepped down off the VLine bus from Melbourne and stretched out the kinks after the five-hour upcountry journey into western Victoria. She looked around, not really expecting that her small country hometown of Mundarra had changed much in her ten-year absence. Strangely, over the last year, she'd been contemplating a possible permanent return to Australia.

Because there were no taxis, she pulled up her suitcase handle and started to walk, wondering if she would meet anyone she knew or if they would even recognize her if she did. It hardly mattered. She was only here for her father's funeral and would soon be gone again.

She shivered in the face of the chill August wind, forgetting, after living in hotter climates for years, how cold it could get. As she turned onto the long main street, Lucy was filled with a surge of familiarity and remembrance. It was as charming as ever. Strong council bylaws ensured that, although interior renovations could be carried out, the historic facades were retained.

Warm red brick glowed in the pale late winter sunshine, ancient gums and shimmering, gold flowering wattles shaded the central parking down the length of the street. Incredibly, most shops seemed the same: the Georgian post office on the corner, the bakery windows filled with luscious delights and squares of award-winning vanilla slice, the smell of still-warm freshly baked bread wafting into her senses as she passed by. Occasionally, a fellow pedestrian smiled or nodded in passing rather than acknowledgment; interested in the odd sight of a suntanned, travel-weary woman dragging a wheeled suitcase.

Carole's hairdressing salon was still across the road. Even as Lucy glanced in that direction, her high school friend emerged into view and came dashing across the street.

Carole frowned then smiled. "Lucy?"

She nodded and each summed up the other after such a long time. Carole was neat as a pin in a long white salon coat, black slacks, and comfortable flat shoes. Her curly, neat wheat-gold hair shone like a halo in the sun around her made-up heart-shaped face. Lucy, on the other hand, was downmarket as always in cargos, a tank top, and sandals. Although, since arriving back to a southern Australian winter, she'd added a warm fleecy jacket.

A moment of awkwardness followed, then Carole stepped forward and gave Lucy a politely restrained hug, more in sympathy than friendship. "We wondered when you would arrive."

"It was a struggle," she admitted. "I borrowed a vehicle to get to Medan, then had a connecting flight to Kuala Lumpur before seven hours of flying onto Melbourne. I'd forgotten the long haul from the city up here by bus." Lucy smiled weakly, privately pleased to see a familiar face but bone weary and longing for a sleep.

Perhaps reading her mind, Carole said, "You must be exhausted. I'll bring around a casserole later. You won't feel like cooking dinner."

Lucy almost crumbled with gratitude at her old friend's empathy. "That's kind of you, but it's not necessary. I'm sure there must be a can of soup in the pantry."

"No trouble. I'll see you later." Typical Carole—maternal and insistent. Lucy smiled to herself as her friend hurriedly crossed the street back to her salon. Her arrival in town would no doubt be fodder for women's gossip under the hair dryer.

At the end of the street, Lucy stopped, her interest piqued by the row of shiny new cars and colorful flags on the corner lot. The entire front of the main building was emblazoned with a huge sign declaring MUNDARRA MOTORS. Wow, Flynn Pedersen had certainly done well for himself. A decade ago, his business had been a small two-pump service station. Now it looked like it had been completely expanded and renovated. It was twice the size, and the formerly empty block next door was now an adjoining new and used car dealership.

Lucy's heart skipped a beat when a familiar male figure strode into view with a scowl on his face and a mobile phone pressed to his ear. With his head bent as he walked, his dark sandy hair flopped appealingly across his forehead. Like it always had. He hadn't aged a day.

Still handsome, in great shape, and still busy making money by the look of it. Before he caught her gaping, she gripped her suitcase handle and trundled past.

But although deep in conversation, as chance would have it, he glanced up. Preoccupied, he looked right through her, then halted mid-stride and stared. Despite the distance, she knew those surprised eyes were steel blue. He acknowledged her presence with the barest nod. Feeling embarrassed, she flashed half a smile in return and waved, picked up her feet, and continued walking, still feeling the cold waves of hostility from his glare.

Without daring to look back, she turned left onto Deacon Street and headed toward the house where she had lived for the first eighteen years of her life. The first pink blossom was appearing on the prunus trees and bulbs were striking through the soil, adding color to gardens. Lucy used to know who lived in most of the homes she now passed, and she suspected most of those same people lived in those same houses. Despite the trend to city migration, due to its stable population, Mundarra somehow survived.

She paused in front of number 24, one hand resting on the gate. The timber cottage had a wide veranda across the front trimmed with decorative scrolled fretwork. It looked sedate and comfortable but, to Lucy, it had only ever been a house, never a home.

Out of habit, she checked the mailbox, finding nothing. It was probably being held at the post office or delivered to the estate lawyers. She struggled to drag her case through the narrow gate opening and walked around to the back door. The cottage plants and bush roses edging the neat brick pathway brushed the bottom of her slacks, and the last of the daffodils nodded their heads in golden clumps. It was a far cry from the summer mud and winter dust underfoot in the poor villages where she worked overseas.

She hoped after all these years the spare key was still in its usual place. On tiptoe, she groped across the door lintel in the garden shed and found it. Lucy wiped her feet on the half-moon coir mat, took a deep breath, and turned the key in the lock.

Stepping inside, she crossed the enclosed porch and stood for a moment in the kitchen, absorbing the silence. Inside were the same outdated pastel cupboard doors that had always been there, the same round table in the middle of the room. All was neat and clean as though someone had just stepped out to do the shopping and would return at any moment. Her father had never lifted a domestic finger his whole life, so she presumed he'd had a housekeeper after her mother had died and his only child had left.

She rubbed her arms against the cold emptiness. First things first. Light a fire and get some heat into this ice box. The wood box was full, so with the living room fire crackling and its heat thawing the chilly rooms, Lucy decided to take a bath. The thought made her positively drool. Hot running water at the turn of a tap. What a luxury. She normally used a bucket of cold water under a camp shower.

Returning indoors, Lucy hauled her suitcase down the wide central hall running the length of the house and into her old bedroom at the front. She glanced at the closed door of her parents' room opposite, knowing she would have to undertake the dismal task of sorting through their belongings. She heaved her case onto the bed, pulled off her sandals, and rubbed her swollen feet. As a special treat and since dinner was organized, she lazed for a long while in a reviving hot bubble bath.

Lucy had only just indulged in her bathing fantasy and changed into a warm, comfy tracksuit when Carole appeared at the back door carrying a hot casserole in a thermal cover. Lucy invited her in and they stood uncomfortably, facing each other across the kitchen table.

"So, you're working in Indonesia?" Carole ventured.

Lucy nodded. "In Aceh for a few years since the tsunami. Before that in Africa and the Pacific Islands."

"I guess you won't be staying long."

"No. Just long enough to clear the house and put it up for sale." She didn't explain the reason why or that she might not be there much longer. Time enough for details later.

"Maybe we could get together for a chat while you're home," Carole suggested.

Lucy's lips twisted into a faint smile. Mundarra *had* been home. Once. But not anymore. With her father's death, she no longer had any ties to the town. She was eager to fulfill her obligations here and leave. Her orphaned children needed her, and she was anxious to return to them. "Sure. After the funeral perhaps?"

Carole nodded. "I'll call around for my dish in the morning." She hastily backed away and left.

Outwardly, her old friend seemed fine, but something wasn't quite right. In working with emotionally damaged families, Lucy had an instinct for sniffing out sadness and despair, and Carole's attitude screamed for help.

After devouring Carole's delicious stew, Lucy felt indulgent. Wearing a pair of mothballed flannelette pajamas retrieved from her old bedroom dresser, she rescued what her mother had always termed the "medicinal brandy" from the pantry and took it into the front sitting room. After stoking the fire, she half-filled a glass with the golden liquid then leaned back to take her first sip. She sprawled over the tapestry couch, wriggling to find a comfortable spot on its hard threadbare surface and clicked the television remote. Even that entertainment, taken for granted here, was a rare delight.

Later, sleepy from alcohol, not to mention exhaustion after traveling from Indonesia, Lucy's body relented and her eyelids grew heavy. The logs in the fireplace had burned down to glowing embers. Too tired to move and add more or prod them into life with a poker, she dragged a crocheted rug over her and curled into a ball instead, almost instantly falling asleep. At some point, her foggy mind registered the front doorbell and persistent knocking. Unable to stir, she disregarded the pounding, snuggled further under the rug, and drifted back into oblivion.

When she woke, it was to the shouts of children playing and caroling magpies somewhere in the garden. She stretched away the stiffness of having slept all night on a lumpy sofa. Beams of sunshine seeped through the open curtains, making patterns on the floral carpet. She gingerly sat up, yawned, and stretched, pushing a handful of long hair off her face.

Instead of dressing, she wrapped up in her robe then took a tray of toast and tea out into the sunshine on the north patio. The wind had dropped since yesterday, and a tepid sun bestowed enough warmth to prophesy spring in the air. The leafy greenery of a climbing rose bush dappled shadows over the lattice shelter above. She'd barely spread her marmalade when her ears tuned in to the rumbling sound of a vehicle pulling up on the street. Sounded like Carole's car needed a new muffler. The latch clicked on the front gate.

"I'm around the side," she called out, expecting her friend as promised, and panicking for a moment when she realized she had only soaked her casserole dish overnight and not washed it yet. Meticulous Carole would be cross.

But it was Flynn Pedersen who materialized around the corner of the house and strode determinedly down the footpath toward her. He halted abruptly, face stern, and braced his hands overhead on the timber beams. "Morning."

"Oh." Lucy sucked in a breath of surprise. "Flynn." Her old flame was still in great physical shape, she noticed. Lucy whipped her long brown legs off the spare director's chair where she'd been sunning them and leaped to her feet.

Flynn masked any surprise, ducked his head, and moved closer. She'd forgotten how tall he was and raised a hand to her eyes, shielding them to look up at him since he had his back to the morning sun. In the seconds it took to size each other up, a wave of nostalgia descended over her for what might have been. As quickly as it rose, she crushed it. Relationships and dredging up the past weren't on her agenda.

Flynn anchored his thumbs into his belt loops. When his big shoulders lifted into a shrug, a lot of muscle strained for freedom inside his cotton shirt. It was hard not to admire or ignore it. "I called around last night but couldn't raise you. I figured you must have gone out."

Lucy recalled the thumping at her front door. So, Flynn had been the mystery caller. After his unfriendly glare yesterday afternoon, she expected she would be the last person he would visit and frowned. "I guess I was . . . sleeping." She felt bad for the lie but she *had* fallen asleep. Eventually. "It's been quite a week."

"I imagine it has," he drawled, eyeing her steadily. "You looked beat yesterday." He'd noticed? "I came by to pay my respects."

"You could have done that at the funeral this afternoon."

"Yes. I could."

"Why didn't you?"

He shrugged. "Just wanted to make sure you were okay. You looked . . . lost. If you need anything . . ."

"I'm sure I'll manage." Wry mockery edged her words.

As Lucy smiled grimly up at him, she noticed his jaw clench with tension or as though he was hurt. It surely wasn't regret that they'd parted on such incompatible terms? From what she'd heard, he recuperated soon enough to marry within months of her leaving.

"How's Sandy?"

He looked away and his mouth pulled into a thin line. "She's . . . ah . . . living with our son, Joshua, in Perth now."

Across the country? Obviously something was not right. Despite the personal animosity that clearly still lingered between them, Lucy's heart genuinely went out to him. Any marital separation couldn't be good for a relationship. She wondered if it was permanent and, perversely, itched to know.

Flynn hesitated but, after an awkward telling silence, eventually admitted, "We're divorced. Have been for a couple of years now."

"I'm sorry," she said softly, and marveled that any woman would desert such a handsome, successful man who also had other admirable personal qualities, as she well knew from dating him during the last two years of high school.

"You staying long?"

She shook her head. "Only as long as necessary. A week or two maybe. I can't spare much time."

'Where are you working now?'

Lucy repeated what she had told Carole and, wisely interpreting his hard glare, didn't bother to elaborate further. Flynn used to be more interested in helping himself than helping others, and that preference had clashed with her desire to do volunteer work overseas with displaced children. This drive stemmed from her own unhappy childhood, she knew, and a desire to give security and affection to those in need.

When Flynn's mobile rang, Lucy felt relieved. He turned away to tersely answer it and hung up. "Needed at the shop." He pointed a thumb over his shoulder. "I'll be getting back."

As he backed away, she predicted what was about to happen, cringed, and lifted an arm in warning, but it was too late. Flynn forgot to duck under the lower sides of the wooden beams above, and he knocked his head with a dull thump.

She clamped a hand over her mouth. "Are you okay?"

He scowled with embarrassment and annoyance. "Fine," he snapped.

She folded her arms and stifled a grin. His pride was hurt more than anything. All the same, she appreciatively eyed his neat backside in jeans as he spun on his shiny leather boots and disappeared from sight. The gate squeaked open and clanged shut, his throaty vehicle roared to life, and the noise faded as he drove away.

Lucy collected her thoughts and, for a second, almost wished he hadn't told her he was single again. It made him available, a potential romantic interest. Except to her, of course. Been there, done that. Didn't work.

Lucy had scarcely finished her toast when a female voice echoed a "*Cooee*" from the front garden.

"Around here, Carole." This time, it was the caller she expected.

"There you are." Her friend's tone held a hint of exasperation. "I knocked front and back and there was no answer." She nodded toward Lucy's half-finished breakfast. "You're starting late this morning." Her tone held accusation. Unlike Flynn, Carole readily made herself at home and sat down in the spare chair Lucy indicated.

"No hurry. The funeral's not 'til two."

"Of course. Roger and I will give you a lift," she instructed.

Lucy ignored her dominance. "That's thoughtful of you. I'd appreciate it."

"We'll come by just before two, then."

Lucy made to rise. "I haven't washed your casserole dish yet. Sorry."

"That's okay. I can collect it another time." Carole waved an arm in dismissal and hesitated. "I was hoping for a private chat. You'll be mobbed at the funeral, I expect, and I might not get another chance when you're busy packing up the house. If you need a hand . . ."

Lucy acknowledged her offer with a nod. "I'll ask." When their conversation flagged again, she said, "It's like Highway One around here this morning. You're my second visitor."

Carole raised her penciled eyebrows. "Yes, I noticed Flynn leaving as I pulled up." She paused. "I guess you'll be renewing a lot of old friendships."

There was that disapproval again, revealed in the sharp edge to her voice. Lucy found Carole's pettiness irritating after living and working among disadvantaged people where more importance was placed on having enough food and water for the day, and a place to sleep. "He was just being friendly. Like you," Lucy pointed out.

"Maybe." Carole drummed her manicured fingers on the table. "You know Sandy divorced him two years ago?"

"He mentioned."

"You two had a thing once, didn't you?"

"A high school crush." Lucy brushed aside the true depth of the feelings she'd once had for him.

"Still no man in your life?"

Carole's taunt, whether intentional or not, hit a nerve, and Lucy reined in her annoyance. "Not at the moment, no." Pride made her hint at the possibility of romance in her life. "But some of my colleagues are close friends. You and Roger still living in the same house?" Carole nodded. "How are the children?"

"Ben and Amy are fine." Carole looked down at her hands. "Raising a family is rewarding, of course, and I love my kids but, sometimes," she paused. "Well, a change might be nice."

"You want to move from Mundarra?" Lucy was surprised to hear it. Her friend had embraced marriage and settled down straight after high school.

Carole shrugged, shifting uncomfortably in her chair. "Everybody dreams."

Lucy had never thought of Carole having dreams. She'd always seemed so hard working and organized and stable. When she had fallen in love with Roger, she'd seemed so happy and content. "Your time will come," was all Lucy could think of to say.

"Easy for you to say. You have all the freedom you want."

Lucy hesitated to point out that her heavy feeling of obligation to the poor communities where she worked gave her anything but freedom. Hers was no nine-to-five job. She became part of village life and all that entailed. She was entitled to holiday breaks but rarely took them. If she did, she usually backpacked to other Third World countries scouting out possibilities for future work.

Despite her dedication, it didn't mean she ruled out a family one day. She'd already made steps in that direction by fostering an orphaned Indonesian girl, Maya.

Perhaps because Carole's sharp comment had drawn

Lucy deep into thought, her friend may have realized it had sounded hurtful and said, "Sorry. I didn't mean it to come out that way."

"No need to apologize," Lucy reassured her. "I guess it seems that way to you. I don't have a mortgage, family responsibilities, but I work hard at what I do. Trust me, every person in Mundarra is living in a palace compared to most villagers I know." She paused. "But I think I know where you're coming from. I've found that life is a series of changes. Something happens to alter the status quo you've known for so long, and you move onto the next stage, often without even realizing it." For some inexplicable reason, an image of Flynn Pedersen crossed Lucy's mind. "Sounds like that's what's happening for you. Maybe your life needs to move in a different direction."

"I shouldn't be discontent." Carole's words were loaded with volumes unsaid.

Sensitive to her friend's despondent mood, Lucy prompted gently, "But?"

"Sometimes everything just gets to be too much and I'd just like to cut and run," she blurted out, darting Lucy a guilty glance. Normally wiry and tenacious, the woman in control, Carole suddenly looked desolate and fragile. "It never stops. There's always something. Everyone seems so dependent on me. I work full time, there's the kids, endless bills." Carole sighed in frustration. "I need Roger to help more, but he strained his back that time."

Good luck with that, Lucy thought. But from memory she knew he could sure swing a golf club all right. Carole should stop making excuses for the weak man she'd married. At the time, their group of friends had all seen it, but lovers wore blinkers or saw the world through rose-colored glasses.

"I wish Roger would help around the house more and step in to help with parenting and some firm discipline."

Roger, firm? As Lucy recalled, he had trouble making decisions. More often than not, she suspected his wife made them for him. Being forced to assume all responsibility was possibly the reason for Carole's dissatisfaction. Over time, that burden must become unacceptable.

Lucy took a deep breath and juggled tactful words in her head. In her work over the years, she'd learned the psychology of dealing with stressed or drunken husbands who beat their wives, families struggling to find enough food to eat, teaching uneducated couples how to respect each other and live in harmony despite their disadvantages. By comparison, it was too easy to look at Carole's privileged life and class her problems as trivial. Lucy knew they were an important indication of upheaval ahead. She saw a vulnerable side of her friend that had never been revealed before. What to say?

"The problem is, Carole, you're too competent. Delegate. Ask for help."

Carole looked horrified at the idea. "I'm a wife and mother. It's my job."

"It's not your job to do everything alone."

Carole waved an arm and gave a watery smile. "I'm being silly. I guess I'm just tired. You'd think I'd be too busy to stew over such nonsense." Carole gave a nervous laugh then grew serious again. "But sometimes the grass seems greener, you know?"

Lucy thought Carole had backed off too easily. Maybe she just needed to vent, borrow someone's ear. Sometimes just talking out your problems helped solve them or at least see them more clearly. "Don't let the family get you down. You'll cope. You always do."

"Frankly, I'm fed up with being the reliable doorstop." Lucy was surprised to hear her admit it. "Oh." She shrugged. "I guess I'll survive, but I wish . . . well, I just wish." Suddenly, as if someone had snapped their fingers, the old Carole was back. She turned officious again, in command, her confidences over. Displaying the chink in her armor was obviously a rare lapse, but now the curtain was drawn again. "That's enough about me. My marriage isn't perfect but few are, right?"

It sounded like she was prepared to compromise. Maybe it was easier that way.

"Life's a constant search for inner happiness, isn't it?" It seemed Carole was struggling to find it in her life at the moment. On occasion, even Lucy thought about the work she was doing, about how much longer she would like to continue and what other options she might pursue in the future. Working among children, she sometimes considered the remote possibility that one day she might even have babies of her own, then crammed down the urge and dismissed it. Marriage was a precarious gamble. Her own parents had been miserable together. Flynn's divorce and Carole's rocky marriage were further evidence of marital struggles these days. And they were only two of her former school friends. What about all the others?

"How did you sleep last night?" Carole asked.

"Extremely well." *Helped along by some good quality Hennessy,* Lucy smiled to herself.

Last night had felt like her own private wake. This afternoon's funeral would be public. The front she would assume for the townsfolk. The nomadic daughter returning to bury a hard man she had always found impossible to respect and love. Lucy cast a blank gaze across the back lawn and garden. The fruit trees were frothy with white blossoms. "Naturally, I feel a certain sadness over my father's death, the passing of a life, but there was never any love lost between us, and most people knew it."

"George was hardly the nicest man on the planet. He was a difficult man to like. You don't have anyone now, do you?" Carole's voice was full of pity.

"You can't miss something you never had." Lucy sighed and drew up her legs on the chair, hugging her knees in a gesture of self-protection. "I hope people don't treat me like an alien while I'm back. Dad was a good age, and it wasn't unexpected. He'd had a heart condition for years, and everyone knew we weren't a close family." Lucy always wondered why. It wasn't simply his sour demeanor. She'd never felt a close connection to him and regretted having no brothers or sisters. She'd asked her mother once why and received the reply, "It wasn't meant to be."

"Are you sure you'll be okay on your own here?" Carole shivered and rubbed her arms.

"Yes." Lucy smiled in reassurance. "There's a difference between being lonely and being alone. Besides, I have heaps to do." She hesitated to confide her burning inner compulsion to remove every trace of George from the house as soon as possible.

Carole rose, her green eyes revealing doubt at her friend's bravado. "We'll see you later, then. About quarter to two?"

Lucy nodded. "Thanks for coming." She unwound her long limbs from the chair and watched her petite friend hurry away.

Chapter Two

Lucy watched her father's coffin being lowered into the ground and tried to feel something for his passing. When it didn't come, she shrugged deeper into the turned-up collar of her long black coat. Ignoring the minister's rote service, her mind wandered, barely seeing the bleak surrounds of the windy fenced cemetery on the edge of town, bordered by towering stands of eucalypts. Their straggly branches barely broke the nasty August wind sweeping across the surrounding paddocks, forcing the substantial crowd to huddle together. Most residents of Mundarra were present, attending out of respect for a man Lucy thought didn't deserve it.

As Reverend Jennings said a final prayer, Lucy studied the shining toes of her black low-heeled shoes, crushing the grass beneath her feet, impatient for the day's proceedings to be over.

Then, thankfully, they were. Reverend Jennings approached, bearing his usual gentle smile. She withdrew her warm hands from her coat pockets to accept his firm grasp. "Thank you, Reverend," she whispered grate-fully.

Lucy moved forward to the graveside and tossed in daffodils from the garden then stepped back, allowing others to follow. Soon, people approached—some she remembered, some she didn't—offering condolences, pressing close. Lucy's cheeks grew stiff from politely smiling.

"Lucy."

She spun around to acknowledge the familiar voice. As Flynn took her hands in both of his, Lucy was alarmed to feel a current of awareness spring into life again, rekindling similar emotions to those she'd felt years ago and again this morning. She swiftly removed her hands and murmured, "Thanks for coming," but found she was still affected by him standing so close, watching her with his frosty gaze. She backed away.

Fortunately, behind and around him were other members of his family, and they pressed forward.

"Anna. Karl." Lucy greeted his parents warmly. Anna hugged her briefly and said, "You must come around for dinner one evening. Flynn mentioned you're only here for a short time."

"I'd like that." Except it would mean confronting their son again.

Eva, one of Flynn's married sisters, emerged from their group, and Lucy beamed in delight at the sight of another familiar and friendly face. After they embraced as closely as they could, Lucy eyed her former school friend's very pregnant tummy and asked, "When are you due?"

"Any day now." As Eva laughed, Lucy experienced a

twinge of envy for her obvious happiness and impending motherhood. "This will be number four."

"Really? I guess I shouldn't be surprised. You always had a room full of dolls. You're a born mother."

"I hope you're still home when she's born. I know how you love children."

How could Lucy politely refuse? It seemed fate was intervening to constantly connect her to the Pedersen family. Ironically, her attraction for Flynn in high school had grown as a result of his sister being one of her closest friends and the girls haunting each other's homes after school.

There was no further opportunity to speak as a cluster of bodies in another group advanced, hands outstretched, sympathetic faces crowding her personal space. Finally, the crowd dwindled, scurrying for the warmth of car heaters and the promise of a luscious afternoon tea in the church hall.

Lucy joined Carole and Roger again, and they all strode briskly back between neat rows of headstones to the car park. Roger opened the car doors for the women and they scrambled in, grateful to escape the icy wind snapping at every inch of bare skin.

Back in town, the church ladies' guild exceeded all expectations with sinful comfort food spread out on two rows of trestle tables down the center of the church hall. Virtually everyone who had attended the funeral was there. It was a further chance to socialize and gossip, with cups of hot tea or coffee the best way to thaw out from the chill.

In between bouts of being besieged by townsfolk eager to renew her acquaintance, Lucy wrapped her hands around a warming mug of tea and surveyed the room. Head and shoulders above the rest, an unsmiling Flynn caught her eye. Disturbed, even at this distance, by a single glance, she looked away.

An hour later, only stragglers remained in the hall. To Lucy's dismay, Flynn was one of them, and he sauntered to her side. Flustered by her confused emotions around him, she dreaded every encounter. Their differences had proved insurmountable before, and his values didn't appear to have changed over the years.

Irritated to still feel anything for the man, she said, "I thought you'd be long gone back to your business."

"It's an opportunity to socialize and network."

"Of course. Business always comes first with you, doesn't it?"

"It's because of my business that I thought I might be able to help you." She raised her eyebrows in long-suffering query. "If you need a car while you're in town, I'm happy to lend you one. Take your pick of any used car in the lot. They're all immaculately clean and checked for roadworthiness. Safe to drive."

"You mean for a helpless woman like me?" Flynn had always hinted that he believed a woman's place was in the home. Lucy hardly fit that mold. Sandy, on the other hand, had been perfect. Gorgeous, dependent, and high maintenance. Together, she and Flynn must have looked the ideal couple. Why then hadn't their marriage survived?

"Helpless is the last thing you'll ever be," Flynn muttered.

Lucy bristled. "You make it sound objectionable."

"Just stating a fact."

"I don't need a car in a town the size of Mundarra," Lucy argued. "They gobble up fuel and spew pollution into the atmosphere. I hope you promote the sale of hybrid vehicles in your business. Global warming's a problem now." When Flynn's mouth edged into a grin, Lucy felt exasperated to be mocked. "If I need to, I'm sure I can resurrect my old bike."

He shrugged. "Suit yourself. My offer stands." He sank his hands into his trouser pockets and turned to leave.

Wanting to ask him something and hating the need, Lucy swallowed her pride. "Before you go." He half-turned back to listen. "Did you notice the guy at the cemetery standing off to one side under the trees?"

"Can't say I did."

Lucy's shoulders sagged in disappointment. "I thought you might have recognized him. He seemed vaguely familiar, but he didn't introduce himself and he's not here." She scanned the hall.

"Someone from out of town who knew George?" he suggested.

"Maybe."

They managed a stiff good-bye and, after thanking the catering ladies, Lucy sauntered the two blocks back to the house. Anxious to return to work at the salon and local community bank, Carole and Roger had already left, since Lucy had told them she would walk home.

That evening, Lucy forced herself to walk down the hallway and turn her parents' bedroom door knob. Standing on the threshold, she felt a pang of sadness at the desolate room and wondered where to start. One logical place was her mother's carved mahogany jewelry box. After Marion's death, George hadn't offered any pieces to Lucy, and she would never have given him the satisfaction of asking him while he was still alive.

Her interest lay mainly in two pieces: the exceptional engagement ring that she had always marveled that thrifty George had ever been generous enough to buy, and an heirloom brooch set with pearls and a small trailing heart and chain that had been passed down through generations of Greenwood women. Marion had owned little else of value but, from the spare details her mother had ever revealed about herself, these had been dearest to her heart, and Lucy desired them as keepsakes. But, although she thoroughly rummaged among the folds of tissue paper, they weren't in the box. She fossicked through dresser drawers and old shoe boxes used for storage in the bottom of cupboards but found nothing.

Lucy sank onto the bed, mystified and disheartened. Surely her father, with age and forgetfulness, hadn't somehow lost or misplaced them? She latched onto an idea. Perhaps he'd left them for safe keeping at the bank. She'd check on her way to the lawyer's appointment tomorrow.

Thrown by her findings, Lucy's mind clicked into neutral. She stripped the bed, emptied the contents of the two cedar wardrobes, and packed up clothes into giant black plastic garbage bags for delivery to the charity clothes bin on Main Street. How she would manage to transport them there she had no idea. Perhaps one-by-one on her old bike?

It was late when Lucy wearily whipped up a fluffy

omelette and ate it in front of the television while she watched the evening news. She was tempted to languish there but knew she must sort through her father's papers before her appointment with Daniel Thompson the following afternoon.

She unlocked her father's roll-top desk, spreading paperwork out on the kitchen table. Her mug of tea grew cold as she scanned bank statements, her attention focused on large regular cash withdrawals made from the newsagency business account each month. She sighed. Another oddity to investigate at the bank tomorrow since there didn't appear to be any receipts or entries in any of his carefully kept accounts.

Anxious for answers to the missing jewelry and unexplained cash withdrawals, Lucy visited the local community bank as soon as it opened the next day.

"Morning, Roger." Lucy greeted Carole's husband at the front counter. He was one of only a few core staff in the small country branch. "I'd like to see John Hudson."

"The manager? Sure." Roger disappeared, returning moments later. "He can see you now. Go right through." He pointed in the direction of a labeled office door farther down.

John, the son of a local farmer, had left the district for higher education, and was one of the rare species who resisted the lure of the city and returned. He rose as she entered. "Morning, Lucy." They shook hands. "Nice to see you again. How's Indonesia?"

Word had certainly spread quickly. "Exhausting, but I love it. I won't keep you long. I have a couple of queries before I go visit Daniel Thompson later about my father's estate."

"Sure. How can I help?"

He indicated a chair, and she sat down. "I'm missing some of my mother's jewelry." Lucy tried to be diplomatic. "I thought my father might have lodged it here for safe keeping. Did he happen to have a safe deposit box?"

John shook his head, and his eyebrows dipped in a frown. "Your father only came in to bank the daily takings."

"I've made a thorough search, but I'll keep looking. I'm sure they'll turn up." She tried to be positive.

"And the other thing?"

"My father made direct debits from his business account, seems to be around the first of each month. Can you tell me what that was for?"

"I'm sorry, Lucy, all accounts of deceased customers are frozen and information not disclosed until after probate is granted."

"Oh, of course." Lucy tried not to be disappointed, having learned nothing about either query and reluctantly rose to leave.

"I'm sorry I couldn't help. I hope you find the jewelry."

"So do I."

Lucy returned home to finish packing up her parents' effects. Then, after a toasted sandwich and a cup of tea, she sauntered down to Main Street toward the temporary rooms Daniel Thompson used as legal offices one day a week when he visited from Riversdale thirty kilometers away.

The small, historic timber building gleamed with a

fresh coat of cream paint and sported a dark green trim around the windows. Lucy turned the ornate brass door knob and entered. Her shoes sank into the plush, plum-colored carpet. The large, shiny leaves of tall potted plants brightened the gray walls and modern black furniture.

Isobel Moyle, the plumber's wife and Daniel's secretary, smiled as she approached. "Hello, Lucy. Daniel's expecting you. Go on in." She indicated an open inner door.

Seated behind a massive well-used desk that half-filled the room, the lawyer was hunched over the contents of an open file, a disheveled suit coat slung over his chair, tie askew, and wavy hair falling across his forehead. He always looked utterly disorganized, but any doubts about his competence swiftly dissolved upon meeting him. His calm voice, competent manner, and flashing intelligent eyes reassured.

"Good morning, Daniel."

He glanced up but, oddly, did not return her smile. "Lucy. Welcome home."

Perhaps because this was an estate appointment, he was being more serious. Rising from the depths of a buttoned leather chair, he moved around to greet her. They shook hands, and he closed the door. "Please, sit down."

She sank into a comfortable padded chair as he returned to his own and swiveled to face her, elbows on his desk, hands steepled beneath his chin. "My sympathy on George's death even though it wasn't unexpected, was it?"

Lucy appreciated his direct approach. Certainly, as

she had confided to Carole, she felt regret at her father's passing, but sentiment played no part in her detached emotions. "No. His heart condition had prevailed for years." She handed over the bulging envelopes she'd brought with her. "That's everything I could find at home. If I've missed anything, I'll bring it in later."

He accepted the package but showed no interest in it. His mind seemed elsewhere. Lucy waited in silence, aware of the ticking wall clock behind him, the ringing telephone, and Isobel's muffled voice in the outer office.

After a long pause, Daniel slowly withdrew a sheet of paper from the open file before him. "This is a copy of George's will." Lucy thought it strange that it wasn't the original. He frowned. "I don't know whether to let you read it or tell you myself."

Lucy grew uneasy. "Tell me what?"

"This document," Daniel said almost distastefully, "contains new and disturbing information. I must warn you, you may find it extremely . . . disappointing." He gazed at her steadily. "Even upsetting."

Lucy's stomach churned. What trouble had her father caused from the grave? She shouldn't be surprised by anything the secretive man did. That much she'd learned from going over his accounts the previous night. "Go on. Just tell me. Not word-for-word. In a nutshell."

"All right," he said gently. "But be prepared for some revelations."

She nodded, listening, and waited for whatever bomb was about to drop.

"The will is dated twenty-five years ago, about ten

years after George and Marion married. In it, you are specifically mentioned by name as *'my wife, Marion McCarthy née Greenwood's daughter, Lucinda Grace.'* He looked up at her sadly. "I'm sorry, Lucy. You inherit nothing."

He waited to let this disclosure sink in.

"What!" Lucy whispered, clenching her hands together in shock.

"All of George's estate," Dan said quietly. "The newsagency business and property, the house and all of its contents in Deacon Street, the car and any cash or investments, goes to his son, Michael George McCarthy."

"His SON?" The announcement struck her with more force than the knowledge that she had just been disinherited.

"Are you all right?" Daniel's voice came to her through the cloud of thoughts crowding her mind.

"Yes." She focused on him across the desk and shook her head, trying to make it clearer and to make some sense out of this madness. "You mean my father had a son. With another woman?"

Daniel nodded. "Apparently."

"Bloody hell." Lucy gaped, speechless. When she regained her voice, she asked, "How old is this son?"

"Twenty-five."

"Five years younger than me. So, this Michael was born after my parents married?" Daniel nodded. "Making my father unfaithful."

"So it seems."

"Why should Michael inherit and not me? Why discriminate?"

"Ah, that's the thing." Daniel hesitated, shuffling papers. "The will and its wording raises doubts as to the legitimacy that you are, in fact, George's daughter."

Stunned, Lucy whispered, "It does?"

"It's been carefully worded, Lucy."

"It has?"

"Yes."

Lucy swallowed hard and took a deep breath, her mind whirling in confusion. "Have you met the son or had contact with him?" The long look he gave her in unspoken discomfort told her that he had. Lucy edged forward in her chair. "Has he been here?"

Daniel nodded.

"Is he in town at the moment?"

"For a few more days."

Suddenly, Lucy's memory flashed back to the stranger at the cemetery, and she understood why the man had looked somehow familiar to her on the day of the funeral. He was, disturbingly, very like George in appearance, which gave alarming credibility to his claim.

"Is he average to tall in height, with dark wavy hair, and wearing a gray checked coat?'

"That certainly sounds like him."

"Where is he staying?"

"Because this is a delicate matter, Lucy, you'll appreciate that I can't divulge that information without his consent."

"Here in town or in Riversdale?" Lucy pressed.

Daniel shook his head. "I'm sorry."

"Well, I want to see *him*. And you can tell him from me—"

"I'm afraid I don't act for Michael, but I can certainly pass on your wishes for a meeting to his Melbourne lawyer."

"That could take weeks," Lucy protested. "I don't have that much time."

"I'm afraid there's more. Michael wants you out of the house as soon as possible."

Lucy gasped. Being penniless was nothing new, but homeless? She wanted to crumble. She'd had such plans. "Whether it's legally mine or not, for the moment, I'm the tenant. Surely I have rights? It was my home for nearly twenty years." She heard her voice rising in frustration.

"I'm afraid he has every right to evict you at a moment's notice. He may be prepared to consider an extension if we put together a case listing your concerns and objections."

"Oh, paperwork, red tape," Lucy blurted out. "That never achieves anything fast." As she well knew from dealing with endless authorities trying to get things done in poor remote communities in an emergency.

"Any contact you have with Michael should be through his lawyer. He paid me a courtesy call because George told him where his will was kept. He's taken the original. This is only a copy."

"Smart work," Lucy muttered.

After a moment, Daniel advised, "You can contest the will, of course."

"If my fath—" Lucy stopped, struck by the alarming realization that this fact was now under a cloud of doubt. When she was able to continue, she said, "If *George*," she emphasized the name with distaste, "never married Michael's mother, then he's illegitimate. Does that make a difference?"

Daniel shook his head. "I'm afraid not. George can leave his estate to animals in the zoo if he chooses. But, as I said, you can challenge."

Her fury rising, Lucy seized on another thought. "If this will was made decades ago, long before my mother's death, that means if George had died first, she wouldn't have inherited a cent?"

"I'm afraid so."

A deep and bitter resentment built up inside her. Not for herself but for the innocent person she considered mostly wronged in all this. Her mother. "God, it just gets worse. How could he do that to a woman who endured his bitterness for over thirty years and waited on him like a servant?"

"Lucy, you've had a shock." Daniel tactfully intervened. "I suggest you take this copy of the will home with you, read it thoroughly, think it through, and come back to me with any questions in a few days. And it's a given that I'll represent you in any negotiations, whatever happens."

"Of course. Thank you," she muttered, still reeling from the will, its revelations, and its consequences. She simply did not have any spare money to challenge a will, and the injustice of it appalled her. Despite the unfairness of it all, Lucy's first thoughts were for Marion. "Thank goodness my mother is not alive to suffer through all this," she said angrily. "That would have been the ultimate insult to a gracious lady who didn't deserve it."

Daniel rose as she did, his face filled with deep and genuine concern. "Take one of my business cards from Isobel before you go. Call me anytime. Even out of hours at home. I'm happy to . . . talk."

His generosity was almost her undoing. Her insides crumpled, but then Lucy remembered the man who had misled both her and her mother and refused to waste one single tear. "Thank you. For everything. I'll be in touch."

Chapter Three

As Lucy stumbled in a daze from Daniel's office, she almost wished she could share the shattering news with someone, but who? Riddled with a deep sense of mortification that her whole life until now had pretty much been a lie, she wanted to be alone, preferably in wide open spaces.

As she walked home the back way along side streets to avoid the possibility of meeting anyone she knew, Lucy bitterly wondered if she should start thinking of it as *the house on Deacon Street* instead of home. She needed to work off her anger and, for that, only physical exercise would do.

In the garden shed among tools and cobwebs, she retrieved her old bicycle only to find the tires rotten and the chain rusted. She sighed. She'd brought her sneakers. It would have to be a jog. She pulled a fleecy hooded jacket out of her suitcase, donned her running shoes, and headed out onto the country road leading south between broad acre cereal paddocks that spread in every direction for miles.

Any other time, the gentle pounding of her feet and sense of invigoration would have been therapeutic. Blue sky. Crisp air. Perfect late-winter day. Thick, green fence-high wheat and barley crops striking higher for the sun that only warmed the earth for a few hours each day before it lowered, and the air cooled in the sting of a twilight chill.

Today it was only a means to an end. How the hell were you supposed to deal with the news that your whole life had been a lie? That the man who you'd always thought was your father probably wasn't. That your mother also knew and had been equally deceptive, and the million questions that this raised. But mainly, how had it all happened and why?

She pushed herself harder and let the cold passing wind whip her cheeks until they were numb. Until she was so focused on the activity that it edged the most turbulent thoughts to the back of her mind. Eventually, she grew exhausted. Lucy estimated she must have covered ten kilometers, having reached the fringes of a small state reserve of protected natural bushland.

She slowed to a brisk walk, then stopped, spinning a 360 degree circle to scan the surrounding countryside and make sure that, apart from birds and sheep, she was alone. Lucy closed her eyes, took a deep breath, and released a long and piercing cry of frustration that hurt her chest and throat. When she opened her eyes again, nothing externally had changed except that a few sheep were now staring at her instead of grazing and some crows had flown to higher limbs in trees. But she felt better for having released some of her anger and frustration.

The grass was cold and damp beneath her as she sat down cross-legged. She pulled her sleeves down over her hands and hunched over her knees.

As the sun drew closer to the horizon, giving way to dusk, Lucy knew she really should be heading back but lacked the energy. She checked her watch. It would be dark in an hour. Her mobile phone nestled in her jacket pocket, but who could she call for an embarrassing rescue? There was always Carole, of course, but after her visit on Saturday morning, it sounded like she had enough to deal with in her own family life at the moment. She didn't want to add her own problems on top of all that. She could stop a passing motorist. Farmers would be heading back out to their homesteads at this time of day.

Even as Lucy tried to muster enthusiasm for the return trek to town, she heard and saw a vehicle approaching, its headlights on low in the fading light. She was about to wave and flag it down when, in astonishment, she recognized the man behind the wheel of a flashy silver four-wheel drive, its radio aerials sticking out on the roof like alien antennae. The car skidded to a halt in the roadside gravel, and the driver lazily got out and leaned against the front bumper, arms and legs casually crossed as though he'd just pulled up for a yarn. Perhaps he had.

"What on earth are you doing out here?" she asked.

"My thoughts exactly."

Lucy waved an arm to encompass the fences, pad-docks, and gum trees. "In the entire district, we both end up on this square patch of dirt. Do you have GPS track-ing me?" When he didn't answer, she added, "I came for a walk. What's your excuse?"

Flynn hedged but didn't respond. He just scowled and ignored her question. "Why didn't you ride your bike?"

"Rusted and gone to bicycle heaven," she admitted sheepishly.

"Why did you come out so far?" He paused, observ-ing her rather too closely for comfort. "Are you okay?"

Lucy plucked at blades of grass and looked away, but she felt him watching her. The silence lengthened be-tween then. Crows cawed, and a rush of evening breeze briefly stirred through the leaves.

"Lucy?" he urged.

The moment had come. She had to tell someone or she'd burst. The kind of revelation she'd been dealt to-day wasn't meant to be buried for long. She needed to share with someone. Though Lucy cursed the irony that it should turn out to be her emotional nemesis, Flynn Pedersen.

She looked across at him, big and comfortable with who he was. Part of a large Swedish family of married siblings plus a tribe of nieces and nephews. And she'd just learned she had nothing. Suddenly she felt inade-quate and couldn't quite bring herself to confess the truth about her own fractured family situation.

"It was nice to catch up with Eva at the funeral."

Flynn eyed her perceptively, and Lucy felt the weight of his puzzled scrutiny, knowing he was aware of her stalling tactics. "*Mor* spends a lot of time with her and helps with the other three.'

Lucy grinned to herself in amusement at Flynn's fond reference to his mother in Swedish. "Eva's looking well. You're lucky to have such a close family."

"I know it." A long awkward silence stretched out between them. "You don't really want to talk about my family, do you? You're upset about something." She remained stubbornly silent. "What's wrong?"

His bluntness was not his most agreeable characteristic but then, she supposed, it got things done. There must be a softer side buried somewhere. Of all people to confide in. She inhaled a deep breath of frustration, disregarded their history, and decided to plunge ahead with both feet.

"I . . . had some upsetting news today," she managed to say eventually.

He frowned and patiently awaited her explanation. It took a moment to let the words gather in her mind and voice them. Suddenly, the years fell away, and she found herself confiding and trusting in this man as she had previously always been able to.

"I found out today that George McCarthy claims he's not my father, and I've been disinherited. I've also been evicted from my house. The woman who could enlighten me is dead too, so, in essence, I have no family and no idea who my real father might be." She looked up at Flynn. "If my name's not McCarthy, what is it? Who am I, and where do I belong?" she appealed helplessly, as if he should know the answer.

His mouth thinned into a soft whistle. Frowning, he pushed himself away from his vehicle to come and sit down beside her. He gathered her cold hands in his own and rubbed them as much for comfort as for warmth. The gesture brought a lump to her throat, reviving past memories, and she longed to dissolve against him but swallowed hard to stifle the inclination.

"*Min Gud!*"

Even though he had been born in Australia, Flynn occasionally lapsed into Swedish, influenced by parents who sometimes still spoke their native language at home. She'd always found his slight foreign accent part of his appeal.

Slowly, she repeated the essence of her conversation with Daniel Thompson, realizing how isolated and alone she had felt since hearing the news, and what a huge relief it was to finally be able to share. Sitting close together, knees touching, hands clasped, Lucy felt as though she was in confession even though none of her present situation was of her making.

"If it's true," she murmured, "I feel the deepest sense of betrayal. From both of them. Oh, I understand my lovely refined mother would have been ashamed to make such an admission, but why couldn't she have confided in me before she died?"

"Maybe there was a good reason."

"I may never know, but what harm could there have been at that point in her life?" Lucy said in frustration. "What purpose could there possibly have been for keeping it secret? I deserved to be told."

"I agree."

She'd had time to reflect on the mystery surrounding her birth and George's deliberate manipulation, not to mention the contrived injustice of it all.

"I always felt guilty because I never liked or respected the man. Now it turns out he might not be any relation to me whatsoever." She glanced at Flynn again, bewildered. "Maybe that's why I never felt any bond with him." The painful irony was not lost on her, and she gave a bitter laugh. "Did he want to punish me because I wasn't his, do you think?" She didn't wait for Flynn's answer. "If he despised Marion so much, why did he marry her? Did he know she was pregnant? No." She shook her head, answering her own question, babbling on. "I don't believe my mother would ever have deceived George. She was too honest for that. She would have told him beforehand. So, presuming she did, why did he marry her and agree to raise another man's child? And why, after all these years, has he suddenly disowned me and brought it all out into the open? A dead man's revenge?

"Oh," she sighed, slipping her hands from Flynn's and streaking impatient fingers through her long hair. "I know they kept company for years, and I often wondered what triggered their actual decision to marry. Seems it was me," she said ruefully. "I was the catalyst for our family's misery."

"Don't think that. You were the result, not the cause."

"I can't help it. I always thought the discrepancy between George and Marion's wedding date and my birth less than nine months later meant I was either a honeymoon baby or premature. And because my mother was such a private, sensitive woman, I never asked." Lucy punched a fist into her palm. "I should have. It might have brought all this out into the open sooner. I would never have dreamed Marion would be an unwed mother.

She was so . . . reserved," Lucy confided. "Maybe that's why my parents were never loving toward each other. They rarely showed affection."

Lucy looked off into the evening gloom where, occasionally, square pockets of light glowed pale yellow in homestead windows. "So, who was my mother's lover?" she murmured, sinking her chin into her hands, emotionally spent, turning aside to see Flynn's shadowed profile beside her, shocked at the compassion in his eyes.

"You won't find the answers tonight. We should head back," he suggested quietly.

Lucy focused, snapping out of her mental fog, becoming more aware of her surroundings again. "Oh, of course," she said apologetically, scrambling clumsily to her feet. "You're a busy man, and here I am, a stranger these days, spilling out my troubles to you."

"I'm happy to listen."

"I'd appreciate it if you treated our conversation in confidence." Lucy felt uncomfortable with her disastrous family situation.

"Sure." He nodded and opened the car door for her.

Lucy climbed up into the comfort of soft leather seats. Flynn certainly traveled first class these days. As they headed back into town, she closed her eyes, feeling detached and powerless. Although it was embarrassing that Flynn of all people should appear to help, it was wonderful for someone else to take control for a change, so she let him. She couldn't see the harm. She was exhausted, she needed a lift home. It was as plain and simple as that.

She woke with a start when Flynn opened the passenger door, and she registered her surroundings. To her embarrassment, she realized she must have dozed off, and they were back in town. Lucy scrambled from the vehicle, still half-awake.

"Sorry," she mumbled, leading Flynn around to the back of the house. He hovered as she fumbled with the door key. "I'll be fine now. Thank you."

"I'm staying."

She raised her eyebrows at his arrogance. "Are you indeed? Why?"

"Because I'm worried about you."

Touched anew by his thoughtfulness, tears pooled in her eyes but, determined to stay strong, she blinked them away. Too tired to argue, Lucy grumbled, "All right. But only for a while." She eyed the Blundstones on his huge feet with a frown. "And you'll have to take those off."

Doing as ordered, Flynn anchored one hand against the door jamb and pulled off his elastic-sided work boots by the back tab. They landed on the floor with a thud. She noticed his gaze as it slid over the neat porch with its forest of potted plants and the pile of garbage bags she still had to deliver to the charity bin.

"I've been going through my parents' things," she offered in explanation as they passed through into the neat kitchen. Heavy-limbed and sapped from her marathon run, Lucy stood in the middle of the room and hugged herself, lost. "I'd love a shower."

"Okay. Hungry?"

She laid a hand on her growling stomach. It had been a long time since her hurried toasted sandwich at lunch, and she'd used up a lot of energy in her jog. "Yes, but I don't have much appetite."

"Fish and chips?"

She snapped him a wry glance. Surprisingly, it sounded wonderful. "That would be great."

"Back soon, then. I'll drop off those recycling bags to the charity bin while I'm out," he offered and disappeared before she could thank him.

Lucy knew it was thoughtful of him but recognized the irony that, of all people to swing by when she was at her lowest, Flynn Pedersen should be the one to be so supportive when she needed it the most.

By the time Lucy had showered, he still hadn't returned. She stoked the sitting room fire, aimlessly prowled the house, and peered out the front window, waiting. Soon enough she heard his sleek four-wheel drive rumble to a stop in front of the house. He used to drive a beat-up old white ute. He'd certainly come a long way.

Mrs. Dawson from across the street would be paralytic with shock and twitching back her curtains to see Flynn haunting Lucy's house. No doubt the gossip grapevine was well underway and telephone lines running hot. Lucy sighed. What did it matter?

What concerned her more was the scandal that would erupt when people discovered her astonishing family situation. And learn they would. In a small town, it was only a matter of time. But rumors spread, and the ultimate disclosure would be unavoidable. Lucy knew she wouldn't be the one to tell them. Yet.

Moments later, Flynn bellowed from the back door, "Lucy, you decent?"

She groaned. She wasn't stupid. She knew their old chemistry still existed because she felt it too, whenever they were together and saw the attraction in his eyes whenever he looked at her. She must work on putting a brake on her feelings for him that had flared up again since she'd come back.

"Come in," she called out.

Flynn gaped at Lucy across the room as he entered, a man's stare for a woman. Aware she was wrapped in only her favorite flimsy oriental robe over silky pajamas and shuffling around in fluffy gray slippers, she grew uncomfortable, feeling dowdy. She'd scrubbed off her makeup and regretted her decision to dress for bed. Just as well, perhaps. It would help squash any romantic presumptions he might have.

"Sorry I took so long," he muttered, finally dragging his gaze away from her to put their box of food on the kitchen table.

Lucy defensively crossed her arms and rubbed them. "I've disrupted your evening."

He shrugged. "I had no plans."

She was more than a little surprised to hear it. Bearing the stigma of divorce or not, Flynn was an extremely handsome man and a good catch. She would have thought local women would be falling all over him.

The food smelled tempting as Lucy ignored having her old high school flame in the house alone with her and unwrapped their simple tasty feast. She deliberately settled into a chair as far away from him in the sitting room as possible. As she ate the flaky fish and licked her salty fingers, she sank deep into thought, unable to stop her mind being drawn back like a magnet to the new facts and realities of her life.

"Penny for them."

Lucy cast a guilty glance at Flynn. "That obvious, huh?" She frowned. "I was just mulling over what I told you out on the road when you found me earlier and wondering why, if Michael was the favored son, he didn't want to participate in George's funeral. Why he stayed in the background."

"Maybe he didn't want to intrude. Or he didn't have the courage."

Lucy scoffed. "If he's anything like his father, I'd be surprised. I'd *like* to think his actions were motivated out of consideration for George's life here in Mundarra and my place in it, but he's keeping himself safely anonymous. A coward's way if you ask me," she muttered.

Flynn shrugged. "He's the stranger here, the outsider. Maybe he never had much to do with George. Maybe Michael's birth was only a means to an end."

Lucy stared at him, horrified at the suggestion, unwilling to believe George would stoop so low. "Surely not. Either way, I need to meet Michael and talk to him. George's claim is only that until proven otherwise, but if his allegation is true, then it means the start of a journey to try and discover who my real father is. Or was."

"Wouldn't it be best to negotiate all this through lawyers?"

"Best for who?" she challenged irritably with a dark glance in his direction.

"Don't get too far ahead of yourself," he warned. "One step at a time."

She knew he was right. But then Flynn had always been realistic and sensible. Grounded. Making Lucy and her own nomadic lifestyle feel inadequate by comparison. "I can't help plotting all the future possibilities to be resolved," she muttered. "My life's just been turned upside down today."

He held up his hands defensively. "Okay. Don't get snitchy. You can't do any more about it all tonight anyway." He stood up, stepped closer, and offered her an outstretched arm. "You should try and get some sleep," he said softly.

"It's still early," Lucy protested, although she appreciated his concern and found his unsought kindness disarming. She refused his hand and rose beside him, stepping around him so he wasn't so close.

"All the same." He frowned. "You're pale. After emotional shock there can be . . . delayed reactions. I'd like to keep an eye on you tonight."

Lucy gaped in surprise. "What are you suggesting?"

"That I stay here."

"Are you making a move on me?" she challenged.

"Not out of the question. You've always been an attractive woman. But, no," he shook his head, and his expression shadowed. "We've learned our lesson, haven't we?"

Hurt by his blunt denouncement, she mumbled, "Yes. Of course," feeling slighted by his easy dismissal. "I'll be fine. I don't plan any hysterics. It would be wasted energy."

"You can never tell."

"It's not necessary, you know," she objected.

"I disagree." He would. When she just stared at him and hesitated, he lifted his big shoulders into half a shrug. "We both know how it's going to look. If you can deal with gossip, so can I. I'm used to it," Flynn said rationally, hands planted determinedly on his hips.

Clearly, he didn't intend taking no for an answer and felt a sense of dishonor for the breakdown in his personal life. That loss would have been difficult enough without the extra blow to his pride.

"Just in case, okay?" he clarified.

Lucy wavered. She didn't see the point or the need. Right now, her world was an unresolved mess. She felt angry and weary and confused. Nothing a good night's sleep wouldn't cure. She guessed it couldn't do much harm if he stayed. Scandal and a tarnished reputation could be endured. She'd always been considered the prodigal daughter anyway, the non-achiever, the dropout. No matter that she was doing valuable, important social work out there in the world.

"I could get Carole instead," Flynn offered.

Lucy panicked. Word would spread all over town that Lucy McCarthy, or whatever her name was, had a breakdown and her friend would want to know why. "No! No one else must know my situation. Nothing's been proved or finalized. It's all speculation at the moment. There's still a lot to be settled." Besides, Carole would fuss and organize, and Lucy couldn't cope with that at the moment. Flynn would just *be* there. Right now, that was enough.

She noticed he was eyeing the shabby sofa. "Not impossible." She managed a grin. "But for no extra charge, I can get you an upgrade. I've stripped the main bedroom, but if I give you fresh sheets, could you make it up?"

"Sure."

Lucy raided the linen cupboard then showed Flynn into the spare room. "Bathroom's that way," she pointed down the hall. "I've put out a fresh towel for you."

"Thanks."

She pushed a hand up into her hair and yawned. "Can you check the door locks? I'm bushed."

He nodded. "Call out if you need me."

Buried under her doona later, Lucy heard Flynn moving about before settling in for the night and thought how strange it was to have him sleeping under the same roof.

Chapter Four

Flynn lay stretched out on his back, still fully dressed, hands clasped behind his head, his bare feet hanging over the end of the bed. He stared at the ceiling in the dark, contemplating Lucy. She was as contrary and beautiful as he remembered, fiercely idealistic too. That trademark silky black hair trailing down to her waist, making him tongue-tied. She'd noticed his stare when, without warning, his old feelings for her had kicked into life again to see her looking all soft and wrapped up ready for bed in her pajamas. But he'd recovered. Feelings he'd never had for Sandy he was ashamed to admit for Lucy. A fresh wave of guilt ran through him that he should never have married Sandy in the first place. Only good thing to come out it had been their son, Joshua.

He shook off bad memories of his ex-wife and focused on Lucy again. She'd suffered a cruel emotional blow today, but somehow he figured she was bottling up her feelings, holding stuff in. Maybe because she'd never had loving parents and known real affection. Lucy's buried feelings were bound to surface sometime and he'd prefer to be around when they did. His gut wrenched to think of her being alone when misery hit. She pretended to be strong but, deep down, he was willing to bet she was hurting and in for a bumpy ride in the weeks to come. She'd need answers, so he'd stick close to make sure she was all right.

Confusion caught in his chest over this woman he'd tried for over a decade to forget and couldn't. Seems she was destined to be part of his life again. At least for a while. He didn't fully understand why the thought should nettle him. They always argued, so he should be grateful the thorn in his side was leaving.

Flynn clenched his fists and wished George McCarthy was still alive so he could beat some morals into the sly old scoundrel. Not a very Christian attitude, but it would sure as hell deliver some satisfaction. Payback for Lucy, and to hell with bruised knuckles. She deserved better. Why did the good ones often end up second best?

Restless, he rolled over onto his side, hauled the comforter up higher around his shoulders and dozed.

Waking hours later, all his senses piqued with a nagging feeling that something wasn't right. Hearing faint noises drifting from Lucy's room, he sat up in bed and swung his legs over the side, listening. The moment he recognized the sound, he leaped to his feet and crossed the hall.

Opening her door, he crept in, groping about in the semi-darkness. He stubbed his big toe on a bed post and curled his foot, wincing in pain, sucking in a deep breath to stop swearing. Hobbling along the bed, he made out the shape of her body in the shadows, curled into a ball, and heard muffled sobbing.

"Lucy," he whispered urgently, bending over her.

He sensed her stiffen at his presence, then turn toward him. "I feel . . . so . . . miserable," she choked out between sobs.

Flynn sat down on the edge of the bed and gathered her into his arms, holding her tight. As her warm body shook against him, racked with weeping, he stroked her hair and wished he could transfer some of her pain. Her familiar scent drifted into his memory and seeped into his senses, and he contemplated what might have been. The maddening truth was they were both so different and incompatible, but that didn't mean he couldn't be here for her as a friend.

His shirt grew damp, but he just kept massaging her back and shoulders, waiting out the storm. It took a while but, eventually, she grew quieter. The sobbing lessened to sniffles and sighs.

"How are you doing?" he whispered.

When he felt her body shake he thought she'd started crying again but when she said, "Sure beats hugging a pillow," he realized she was giggling. "Please don't turn on the light. I'll look a mess."

"Never."

As she pulled away from him, her silky hair drifted through his fingers. "Thank you," she whispered, wiping her damp cheeks with the back of her hand.

"You're welcome," he murmured, fishing one of his big, laundered and folded handkerchiefs out of his pocket and handing it to her. "Want me to stay a bit?"

She shook her head and blew her nose. "I'll be fine now."

"I'll leave your door ajar, okay?" Flynn pushed himself to stand.

"Night," she mumbled as she settled down again while he gingerly found his way out of her room and groped his way back across the hall.

The next morning, still drowsy, Lucy was vaguely aware of a deep male voice somewhere not too far away. Waking more, she opened one eye to faint light and lifted herself up onto one elbow. The red numbers on her digital clock said it was barely seven.

Glancing across the room, she noticed Flynn standing in her half-open doorway, an overnight growth of stubble on his chin. Wearing jeans and a dark T-shirt, he clutched his sweater in one hand and held his boots in the other. Suddenly, the memory flooded back of how he had held her last night when she'd broken down.

"Morning. Sleep well?"

Lucy shook herself from her lapse. "After my outburst?" she admitted sheepishly. "Wonderfully." She yawned and stretched.

He hesitated. "I made breakfast."

"You did?" It was more than anyone had done for her in a long while, and she almost burst out howling again in gratitude. Instead, she swallowed back the emotions, surprised at her lack of composure. She'd dealt with tougher situations than this. In her work, she usually managed to stifle her emotions at the constant sadness of poor people's lives and just get on with it. But here in

Mundarra, with all that had happened, she felt strangely vulnerable since her return. "Thank you."

"See that you eat it," he growled and edged toward the front door. "I open up the business at seven."

"You've already eaten?"

"I'll get something later." He waved a hand vaguely in the air. "No need to see me out."

Lucy hesitated only for a heartbeat then sprang out of bed and pulled on her robe. In the chilly morning, it made more sense to stay snuggled under the covers, but her strict upbringing and manners won out, and she ushered him to the front door, holding it open. As they stepped onto the front veranda, the damp frosty air nipped around her bare neck and feet, and she shivered.

"Thanks for being here for me last night and staying," she said to his bent head and broad shoulders as he balanced on each leg and slid his feet into his boots. "I appreciate it." *And so will the town gossips*, she sighed internally.

He straightened and met her gaze. "No problem. Any time." He paused. "Catch you around."

He took the three steps down to the pathway in one giant stride, slammed the gate after him, and climbed into his vehicle. It rumbled into life, condensation from its cold engine rising into the still early morning air, and she watched it chug slowly down the street.

As she turned to go inside, Lucy's shoulders sagged in dismay when she caught Violet Dawson at her mailbox supposedly collecting her newspaper, glaring wide-eyed across the street. The woman was like an unwelcome apparition.

Defiantly casual, Lucy pushed her hands into her robe pockets, smiled, and called out gaily across the street, "Good morning, Mrs. Dawson." She knew what it looked like and didn't care. She had bigger problems on her mind than petty gossip. Her neighbor managed a stiff nod, turned on her slippered heels, and scuttled indoors. As Lucy went inside, she sighed. The bush telegraph would soon be well under way.

To her pleasure, she noticed Flynn had stoked the sitting room fire and its warmth filtered into the kitchen. She stood in the doorway and gaped at the disaster he'd left behind on the countertops. All this for juice and toast? She shook her head and tuned into the radio news, leaning against the bench while she ate. Drinking a steaming mug of green tea, she mulled over the future. There were so many unknowns ahead.

She spent the next hour procrastinating, wanting to meet her father's illegitimate son and satisfy her curiosity but daunted by the prospect. In the end, she started telephoning the local hotels and motels, inquiring if Mr. McCarthy was in. At the Railway Hotel, her third try, she got lucky and the receptionist offered to put her through, but she declined and hung up.

Lucy wondered why he had stayed in Mundarra and not returned to the city. She *must* meet him face-to-face. She needed to assess the measure of the man; find out his reaction to his inheritance and if he'd known about it prior to George's death. How much contact had he had with his father, if that was ultimately proven to be what George was? For her own peace of mind, she needed answers to questions. She didn't care what the answers were. It was just vitally important she knew so she could resolve the fractured pieces of her life and move on.

She was prepared to listen to anything he had to say for himself, assuming he was prepared to accept her visit and answer her questions.

Mundarra's Railway Hotel was a large single story cream-painted timber structure with wide verandas all around. Built near the station for passengers' convenience in the heyday of rail travel, these days, only the inter-capital city train running between Melbourne and Adelaide stopped morning and evening on alternate days. It was also the major long distance bus stop where she had arrived only a few days before.

Lucy bypassed the locals in the bar drinking and playing pool and headed for reception. She politely asked for the room number and wandered the wide red-carpeted hallways until she found it. Without giving herself time to turn and run, she knocked on the door loud enough to be heard above the sound of the television coming from the other side and waited.

When the door opened, Lucy drew in a sharp breath. It was the man she'd seen from a distance at the cemetery. At close range, he eerily resembled George. With a confronting jolt, she realized that the allegations were probably true. He had the same thin face, same crop of dark hair. Without any need for introduction, each instinctively guessed the identity of the other.

Lucy spoke first. "Michael McCarthy?"

His lips curled into an unflattering twist. "Lucy."

She noticed he didn't mention her surname. Discomforting but apt. She had no idea either. Clearly, judging by his sour expression, her presence was unwelcome but perhaps not unexpected. Lucy knew she would waste no more time here than necessary.

"We need to talk." He glared at her with disdain. Not intimidated, she added, "It won't take long."

Reluctantly, he moved aside so Lucy could move past and into his room. An ashen-haired woman in black, tailored slacks and a silky blouse lounged on the bed and scrambled to her feet, darting a questioning glance at Michael.

As their eyes locked, Lucy was distracted by the glitter of her jewelry. Pinned to her ivory shirt she recognized her mother's heirloom Greenwood pearl brooch. Lucy's heart pounded with shock. Speechless, she forced her gaze lower to the woman's hand where a familiar and magnificent diamond ring sparkled over her manicured nails. Gripped with resentment, Lucy clenched her fists, her nails digging into her flesh. Realization hit her that, despite George knowing they were his wife's heirlooms meant for Lucy, he had clearly overridden her right to them.

During her stunned silence and without the courtesy of an introduction, Michael ordered the woman, "Leave us alone."

Without hesitation, she snatched up a handbag and shoes, trotting obediently out the door, closing it quietly behind her. Presumably his wife. The McCarthy men certainly chose dutiful women.

"Don't touch anything in the house," Michael growled. "It's all mine."

Lucy stiffened and permitted herself a Mona Lisa smile. "Not necessarily. Proof needs to be established.

DNA tests." She wasn't prepared to concede everything just yet.

"I want you out of my house."

"It's not yours. Yet. And never forget that possession is nine-tenths of the law. I'll leave when your legitimacy is proved and not before."

"I'll take out a court order."

"Be my guest." Lucy didn't flinch. She had nothing to lose. She'd already lost everything. Her family, her sense of identity. Roots.

"You won't win," he gloated.

"Maybe not." Lucy shrugged, astounded by the man's arrogance. "But I'm contesting the will." In fact, she had decided no such thing. But since meeting this sad excuse for a human being that George had apparently sired, she could at least make it as difficult as possible. "And the wheels of justice do tend to grind rather slowly, don't they?"

Michael glowered and shuffled, rattled by Lucy's forthright honesty and quiet poise, less cocky than he'd been five minutes earlier. "You're wasting your time. I'm his heir. Not you."

"Whatever the outcome, it could be quite some time before anyone inherits anything."

"I *will* inherit," he said with less conviction than she believed he felt. "And I can wait."

"I hope so." She hesitated. "Did you know you were George's heir?"

He barked out a short smug laugh. "Of course."

Lucy winced. "How long?"

"Since birth. Mother made sure." He smirked. "She's a clever lady with *business* deals."

And her blood runs through your veins, Lucy thought. Hardly flattering.

"And this *was* a business deal." Michael sneered. "George just walked up to her in a bar and said he wanted a son and offered her a proposition."

For revenge because Marion became pregnant with another man's child? Any last shred of respect she may have had for George fell away at this last, horrifying ultimate betrayal. Flynn hadn't been so wrong after all.

She sucked up her private anguish and forced herself to ask, "Did you and your mother have much contact with him?"

"Rarely. There was no need. He got what he wanted. So long as he paid us regularly, we didn't care."

The cogs of Lucy's brain clicked into place. The regular payments withdrawn from the newsagency account. And they'd been substantial sums. George's guilt money. Another mystery solved.

"You blackmailed him?"

Michael's gaze narrowed. "He offered."

"Indeed? Generous of him. Don't expect the same from me."

He jerked a thumb toward the door. "Out."

Lucy smiled sweetly. "My pleasure." She moved in that direction, her hand curled around the knob as she turned back to face him. "One last thing. I couldn't help admiring your wife's jewelry."

He sank his hands into his pockets and puffed out his chest, more comfortable now their meeting was about to end. "A wedding present two years ago from *my father.*" He emphasized his last words.

She ached with a deep sadness. George had known they were Greenwood heirlooms and, as Marion's flesh and blood, Lucy's entitlement by moral if not legal right. Now, she lost hope of ever claiming them as her own and having any meaningful keepsake of her mother.

"There'll be more where that came from," Michael was saying as she refocused on their conversation. "Nothing but the best from now on."

"Oh?" Lucy couldn't resist faking interest to learn more. The young man was as stupid as George was sharp.

"New house. New car. And we're organizing passports for world travel."

How simple was this guy? Did he know how low property prices were in a small country town? Turnover hardly made your head spin. Easy enough to read Michael McCarthy's future. Money would trickle through his fingers like dry Wimmera soil in summer, and be gone.

"How wonderful." She doubted he was smart enough to detect the sarcasm in her voice.

As Lucy strode back along Main Street toward Deacon, she shook from the strain of the unpleasant meeting. *That weasel. . . . That miserable yellow . . .* Foul enough words didn't exist to describe George McCarthy and his shallow son. To hell with the money. She didn't want any and wouldn't touch it even if it was offered. Her bigger and more immediate concern now was the question hanging over her paternity. If George wasn't her father, who was?

As she passed Carole's hair salon, Lucy realized her mistake too late when her friend waved madly from inside and rushed out.

"Morning."

Looking alarmed, Carole flashed her a cheesy smile and pulled her toward the edge of the pavement away from the passersby.

"What's up?" Lucy strung her friend along. As if she didn't know.

"Violet Dawson's in for her weekly shampoo and set." Lucy patiently waited to hear the distorted grapevine version. "She barely sat down before she told me about you and Flynn."

Lucy pretended to be surprised. "Oh? What about us?" She couldn't resist some harmless fun.

"You know." She lowered her voice confidingly. "That he was at your place last night. All night," she emphasized, her eyes bulging.

Lucy looked her straight in the eye, all innocence. "Yes. Scandalous, isn't it?"

She deliberately didn't elaborate, and Carole itched with curiosity. Lucy prickled with irritation. Even a friend was willing to believe the worst. Still, it proved entertaining, watching reactions over what only she and Flynn knew to be an innocent evening.

"Well?"

Lucy raised questioning eyebrows, remaining deliberately silent.

"Lucy!" Carole hissed. "Don't be thick. What's going on? Are you two getting back together?"

She resented the need to do so but explained what had happened the night before. That she had been upset, although not the real reason. She let Carole think it was grief.

"You could have called *me*." Carole sounded peeved. "You could have stayed with *us* overnight."

Lucy shrugged. "I know, but Flynn just arrived and offered."

Carole looked dubious and muttered, "As long as that's all it was."

"Why?"

"Well, you two never got on, did you? You don't suit each other. You're two totally different people. I mean, you're swanning around poor countries helping homeless kids and living like a pauper, and Flynn's building an empire and basking in material wealth."

Lucy cringed to hear it put quite so bluntly, but Carole's crude description of their different lives only served to emphasize the gulf between them.

"Flynn seems to be rather attentive all of a sudden, don't you think?"

Lucy ignored the insinuation and gritted her teeth, deciding to be positive. "Yes, he's been very thoughtful."

"He has no chance if he's hoping to team up with you again, has he?" Carole chuckled, leaning closer. "You know him. You won't be fooled by his suave Mr. Nice Guy image."

Lucy debated Carole's comment in her head. She'd seen a more considerate side of Flynn recently. All the same, Carole's warning gave her cause for thought. Despite his attentions seeming genuine, he *had* always watched out for number one. His inflexibility had been a major cause for their parting all those years ago. He had doubted Lucy's work would ever provide her with financial security, and he was right. This time around, he seemed more accepting of the life she had chosen.

"Well, just remember people are talking," Carole warned smugly. "You have a reputation at stake."

"Since it's *my* reputation, let *me* worry about it," Lucy said lightly. "I'm thirty and world weary," she was amazed to hear herself admit. "A little attention might be nice."

Carole looked horrified. "Within reason. Not scandal. You're an attractive woman. You're not that desperate yet, surely. I'd be giving Flynn Pedersen a wide berth," she advised primly.

Ah, but you're not me. Lucy felt a twinge of exasperation, knowing she'd always thrived on a challenge, sought adventure, pushed her personal boundaries. Personally, she thought it helped make you a stronger and better person, not to mention keeping life interesting. Whereas Carole had settled for conventional.

"Well, Flynn's been genuinely supportive, and I didn't ask for his help. He offered." Which was more than most other people had done. She realized that being away for such a long time created distance and perhaps wariness for townsfolk to approach her. Except Flynn. Lucy knew she was beginning to feel dangerously comfortable around him again and not unaffected by his good looks and charm.

For some puzzling reason, despite his busy workload, he always seemed readily available. She hadn't questioned it or given it much thought. Should she feel flattered or had she been skillfully charmed?

Distracted, Carole glanced toward her salon window. "I'd better get back. I hope you know what you're doing but, if it all turns sour again, don't say I didn't warn you."

Chapter Five

"You realize what you're considering will cause a delay in settling George's estate?" Daniel Thomas tented his fingers as he rocked back in his leather chair and eyed Lucy across his cluttered desk.

"I need to know, Daniel. I can't just take George's word for it in the will. Otherwise I'll always wonder and have the doubt hanging over my head for the rest of my life."

Since meeting the odious Michael McCarthy, Lucy needed to settle the paternity issue.

"Of course."

"And you'll negotiate for me to stay in the house until the DNA results come in and Michael is proven to be George's son?" He nodded. "It will buy me some time." At least it meant she had a roof over her head a while longer until all the issues were resolved. "I need to make a stand, Daniel. I have a moral if not a legal right."

He nodded, listening. "Certainly."

"My only concern is how I'm going to pay for it." Lucy contemplated her meager savings.

"The estate usually bears the cost of the challenge."

"Really?" Rapt to hear such unexpected and timely good news, Lucy's heart raced with relief and she felt like leaping across the desk to hug him. Good. Pleasant thought, reducing Michael's inheritance.

"In this document." Daniel waved the will copy. "George has specifically named Michael and yourself and explained his reasons for the disinheritance. He's had excellent legal advice that will make your challenge difficult."

"But not impossible, right?" Lucy pressed, concerned only about the principle involved here, not the money.

Daniel leaned forward and shuffled through some papers. "Since his will is dated only weeks after Michael's birth and George is clearly named as the father on the birth certificate, and you've related your conversation with Michael, the document is unlikely to be overturned." He paused. "It's valid in all respects, and clearly shows George's planned intentions."

Mildly deterred, Lucy's shoulders sank. "Fair enough. All the same, let's wait to see their response." She pulled a wry smile, determined to fight on principle.

"I'll need you to sign a letter of authority to Mundarra Medical Center giving permission as probable next of kin to take a sample of George's blood from his previous heart tests. They won't release it without it. You'll need to give a blood sample at pathology too, and the DNA laboratory will arrange collection of both by courier."

Lucy took a deep breath. It was actually happening. "I'll make an appointment."

"I presume Michael and his mother will give their samples in Melbourne. I'll correspond with his lawyer about that."

Lucy had no problem with any of it. She just wanted the process underway and results found so she could move on to the next step. If necessary. Finding her father's identity.

"How long will all this take?"

"A few weeks. I'll see if I can get some priority placed on your results."

Lucy's spirits slumped. All these hiccups were causing delays and keeping her in Mundarra. She despaired she'd ever get away and back to Indonesia. She was missing her foster child, Maya, more than she would admit.

During the week, Daniel Thompson mailed out the letter of permission for the medical center to release previous blood samples to test George's DNA. Lucy signed it and handed it in when she gave her own sample a few days later.

In her heart, she knew the outcome but feared actually being told. It would seal the fact forever that George had never been her father. Then would come the search for the man who had already been the cause of many restless nights. What if she never found him? What if he was already dead?

As she walked home again, Lucy strolled past Mundarra Motors. She didn't have to come this way. She could have taken another route, but the temptation was there. Of course, as luck would have it, at that moment Flynn appeared from inside the main building and shook hands with a client. She had to admit he looked good and her attention followed him as he roamed about the lot. She allowed herself a brief lingering stare, caught off guard when he suddenly spied her and approached.

His easy smile warmed her heart and she gave herself a mental shake. *Focus, Lucy. You're leaving town.*

"I'm an uncle again," he announced proudly without preamble. "Eva had a baby daughter at Riversdale Hospital last night." His face positively glowed at the news as though he was the father himself.

"Wonderful. Are they both well?" He nodded. "Have they named her?"

"Hanné." He held her gaze like a challenge. "You should come around to see her. She'll be out of Riversdale Hospital in a few days and they're staying with my parents."

"I'll keep it in mind." Her insides melted at the thought of a soft new human being born out of love. She doubted her own arrival into the world had been so welcomed and an ache of privation weighed on her chest.

As she made to walk away, Flynn stopped her by asking, "Do you like movies?"

She did and nodded, guessing where his question was leading. Her hopes rose at the possibility. "Sure."

"The monthly screening is on again this weekend. Would you like to go?"

It was a big evening in town organized by the local progress association. Most people turned out in support to help raise funds for local community projects. She hesitated, fighting refusal and considered Flynn's willingness to spend time with her.

"All right," she agreed. "For old times' sake."

He studied her seriously. "Fair enough."

She shouldn't, of course, but Flynn had always been a magnet and his attraction hadn't lost any appeal.

That evening, she panicked over what to wear. Against her will, she wanted to look good for Flynn. Rummaging madly in the depths of her old wardrobe and emptying out its contents, she retrieved clothes she hadn't worn in years.

When Lucy opened the front door for Flynn, her first thought was *looking good*. Black jeans and a blue denim shirt topped with a fleecy-lined black leather battle jacket. The outfit created a wilder and sexier image than usual. His sandy hair was smoothly brushed back and he dug his hands into his coat pockets, as though they were safe there.

His gaze landed on her and stayed, and his eyebrows flickered up and down in mock mischief making her feel very much a woman.

Flynn swallowed back his astonishment and stared. He was so used to seeing Lucy in jungle greens, it was a shock to run his gaze over the stunning woman before him in a soft-looking purple sweater that hugged all her curves and a pair of tight black slacks. Big dangly earrings were half hidden amongst all that long dark hair swinging around her shoulders and halfway down her back.

She seemed taller until he realized she was wearing high heels. For a woman who'd hinted she just wanted to be friends, Lucy McCarthy was sending out a confusing message. In school days, Lucy had been a classy black-haired angel. He sent up a silent prayer that fate had steered their lives together. For now. However long it lasted, he planned to soak it up. He jammed his hands deeper into his pockets to keep them under control and eyed her with awe instead.

"Evening," he drawled. She looked nervous so he flashed a grin for reassurance. "You look nice."

"Don't sound so surprised." She sounded prickly and defensive.

"Let's not argue."

"That would mean being nice," Lucy quipped wryly.

"I'm willing to try if you are."

Lucy accepted his extended hand and allowed herself to be led to his shiny four-wheel drive, amazed by his warm firm grip and the security it silently conveyed.

Every car in town was parked within a block of the Mechanics Institute on Main Street and a line of people extended from the ticket booth out onto the footpath. As they joined the queue, more than a few heads turned to see Flynn and Lucy together, although few would remember they had once been an item in high school.

Lucy scanned faces for any sign of Carole and Roger's family. Unless they'd arrived early and were already inside, they hadn't come. A shame because this was one of those great chances Carole complained about for the two of them to be together, and it looked like they hadn't taken it. She was probably ironing while Roger was parked in front of the television.

Jostled by the crowd, Lucy fell against Flynn. As if a reflex, he slid an arm around her waist in a protective gesture. Once inside, Flynn sought her hand again, but she tactfully edged away, smiling politely instead as they took their seats. Had she been wrong to dress to please? Encouraging Flynn's interest and rumors? Scary truth was, she wanted to be with him, so she decided to settle back and enjoy the night.

The hall was packed and noisy, people already dipping into boxes of popcorn and rustling sweet packets before being plunged into darkness.

The movie was great. Not just because she hadn't seen one in years but because it was nonstop adventure with a touch of romance. Lucy held her breath at terrifying moments, laughed at the humor woven throughout, and swallowed back soft-hearted tears when moved. At those times, Flynn leaned in closer, their shoulders touching, as if perceptively sensing her tender mood. Rather contrary to the cool public image he usually conveyed.

Afterward, out in the chilly air, young people swarmed in circles to chat, others said hasty good nights, and the crowd gradually dispersed. Lucy and Flynn piled back into his vehicle, shivering and eager to get the heater going. Flynn revved the engine and let it run for a while, spreading welcome warmth into the car before slowly driving Lucy home.

As they pulled up outside the Deacon Street house, she considered asking him in for a hot drink but decided against it. Instead, with one hand on the door knob, she murmured, "It was a great movie. Thanks for asking me. I enjoyed it."

He leaned across and opened her door, bringing them close. "I'll walk you in," he offered, jumping out and striding around to her side before she could disagree.

"I'll be fine," she assured him as she scrambled out.

"You shouldn't be out alone," he murmured.

Lucy chuckled. "In Mundarra? You're kidding."

Under the shadowed privacy of the front veranda, Flynn removed his jacket and draped it around her shoulders, its inner fleece still warm from his body. "I don't really need this," she argued even as she snuggled into it. "I won't be out here long."

"Depends."

"On what?"

Catching the lapels, he gently tugged her closer. "On whether you let me kiss you."

"Oh. I don't know if—"

But she didn't resist when he smothered her protests and their lips met. She enjoyed it but thought of a dozen reasons why she mustn't let it happen again. Lucy stepped back and cleared her throat. "I guess you want your jacket back now."

"You might be surprised what I want, Lucy," he murmured. "Keep the jacket. I'll fetch it sometime."

Inside the house, Lucy closed the door and heard Flynn drive away, not altogether sure she knew what was happening with him. As always, he made her feel special and wanted, but falling for him again would be insane, wouldn't it? They lived their lives on different continents. But in the light of the deep warm kiss they'd just shared, he certainly wasn't holding back from letting her know he was still attracted.

To complicate matters, Anna Pedersen telephoned

the next day inviting Lucy to their family dinner Wednesday night. Without giving her time to object, she announced that since Lucy didn't have any transport, Flynn had offered to drive her around the lake to their home. Since it all seemed arranged, Lucy felt powerless to refuse. Besides, she was growing excited and eager to see Eva's new baby.

Flynn landed on Lucy's doorstep feeling surprisingly happy. Since his divorce from Sandy and rarely seeing his son, Joshua, he'd flung himself into work and community groups to escape his personal loneliness. So, having Lucy back in his life was a refreshing bonus. He'd been surprised how his old feelings had kicked so easily into gear since her arrival. The flicker of chemistry had swiftly reignited between them. He was sure Lucy felt it too. After all, she had returned his kiss the other night. After the first one was so fantastic, he'd wanted to do it again but held back for Lucy's sake, not wanting to rush her. It was early days. She'd be in town a while yet.

So he jumped the front steps in one leap and pressed the bell. As usual, whenever he set eyes on Lucy again, it was like old times, as though she had never gone away, and his heart felt lighter. He'd never deny she had always been good for him. When she smiled, words failed him. Pity they had lived and worked thousands of miles apart. He wasn't prepared to despair just yet. Life had a way of working things out.

A pink jumper sat on her tiny waist and looked as downy as month-old chickens. "Evening." He tried to sound casual and unaffected.

"Flynn," she replied, equally cool. "Your mother will be wondering where we are."

Because he was a few minutes late, he took the jibe on the chin. Fair enough if Lucy was wary. He'd been critical after high school of what he'd seen at the time as her lack of ambition. Back then, he hadn't fully understood her humanitarian goals. He'd had his own agenda and they'd gone their separate ways after a stormy split. A huge mistake he'd lived to regret.

Although he'd kept up with her movements over the years through his sister, Eva, one of Lucy's best friends, he'd had no personal contact with her ever since. Until now. Which is why it had been such a jolt to see her more mature and beautiful than he remembered. She radiated a kind of settled poise, as though she knew where she was in life. Which he found admirable but daunting because he needed to figure out how best to earn her trust and respect again.

Lucy had moved on past him, so Flynn followed her down the path to his four-wheel drive. From behind, he noticed her jeans fitted so tightly they looked like a second skin. And high-heeled shoes. He liked that. It made her look so feminine, as did her lovely hair swinging free all the way down to her waist. But he still thought she was too skinny.

When Lucy saw all the cars parked in the driveway and on the street in front of the Pedersen house, she wanted to leap out of the vehicle and scamper home. As Flynn opened the door and she slid out, she hoped his family didn't misinterpret their friendship. She felt a strange sense of *déjà vu* upon re-entering the house after so long. It reminded her pleasantly, she discovered, of former happier times.

The moment Lucy walked into the Pedersen kitchen, she noticed the difference between her memories of her mother's neat, sterile atmosphere and this large one, bustling with warmth and noise and welcome. She breathed in the familiar aroma of bay leaf and spices of Anna's famous Swedish beef stew that she'd eaten before on more than one occasion.

The older woman stood at the stove, her back to them, and turned around to smile at their arrival. Because she only came up to his shoulders, Flynn slid an arm around his mother and kissed the top of her head. Her gentle face and comfortable build matched her nature. Right now, her faultless complexion was flushed from cooking and strands of graying hair escaped from its usual neat bun.

Anna's warm eyes were silently observant. "Lucy, we're so pleased you could join us." She stepped forward in greeting. "This is my grandson, Tommy, Kristina and John's boy." She regarded him fondly as he clung shyly to her skirt.

"Hi, Tommy."

"Hello."

Flynn ruffled his nephew's blond hair. "How's my little farmer?" Tommy chuckled and scampered away.

"How are you coping since your father's death?" Anna inquired, refreshingly honest.

Lucy flinched at the word *father.* "I'm doing fine. Thanks for asking." If only people knew. "Flynn's been really kind." Lucy felt guilty for being evasive, especially with the Pedersens who had once been like a second family, but her sense of inferiority and shock over her fractured family situation kept her wary.

"He's a good-hearted man." Anna agreed, glancing between them. "Now you two go into the lounge."

"Can I help?"

"No, no," Anna protested. "You're a guest. It's all done. We're just waiting for John to come in from the farm, but the girls and all the children are here. Go and say hello to everyone. You know them all."

Flynn and Lucy wandered through into the lounge, greeting the menfolk deep in conversation in comfortable chairs by the crackling open fire, probably deliberating on the dry farming season and potential yields. Flynn's father, Karl, and his brothers-in-law Stewart and John all shook hands, then Flynn stood back and introduced Lucy to them all. A decade ago they hadn't yet been a part of the family.

Seeing them all together, their Swedish ancestry was evident, the smooth pale skin and blond features. They all hugged her warmly. Karl, pipe in hand, offered her a drink.

New mother, Eva, sat nearby with Hanné a sleeping pink bundle in the bassinet to one side.

"Hi, Lucy. Come see the newest addition to our family."

Lucy bent over Eva and her sleeping baby. She peered down at the tightly wrapped bundle in the baby capsule. "Is she doing well?"

"Sleeps through anything. With three others," Eva laughed, "I'm grateful."

Kristina, Flynn's oldest sister, looked up from their chatting and smiled. "It's nice to see you again, Lucy."

Nieces and nephews scampered in and out at will from the adjoining playroom. Flynn's oldest nephews, Ritchie and Tommy, played computer games; Jenny and Julianna watched television in one corner.

"Hey, Uncle Flynn," they chorused when he poked his head in the door.

Eva's youngest, Matti, knocked into Flynn's legs as he toddled past. "Hey, buddy." Flynn hoisted the little fellow up for a hug, then looked around the room.

Surrounded by noise and tolerance and affection, Lucy experienced a rare moment of envy. Such a difference in the close Pedersen clan, she reflected, sipping her wine, from the chasm that had existed in her own home. She saw how the happy half lived and glimpsed what she had missed. It hadn't seemed so noticeable when she was younger, but in the light of recent developments in her own life, this family now all looked so secure and happy. She began to feel a little lost, aching with a sense of isolation.

She adored children and hadn't completely abandoned the hope that one day she might have a family of her own. Lucy glanced across at Flynn, deep in conversation, and pulled herself together. She refused to dwell on what could have been.

Anna bustled in with the first of the large food dishes. A tureen of pea soup, followed by Swedish meatballs, potato dumplings with homemade crisp bread, and bowls of vegetables from Karl's garden.

Everyone randomly took seats at the long table, Karl

at the head, Anna by his side, Matti swinging his stubby legs in the high chair between them, apparently his regular place. There was a general passing around of plates, spooning out of food, smiling faces, and chatter.

Conversation ranged from Julianna's day at school to John's reduced crop expectations on the farm, a recent fishing trip Flynn had apparently taken with mates—surprising Lucy yet again to learn that he spent any time away from the business—and the coming season in Karl's extensive vegetable patch.

When prompted, Lucy briefly spoke about her work with UNICEF in Indonesia, understating the more distressing aspects she encountered and enthusing at length about her foster child, Maya. She noticed Flynn listening closely as she spoke about the orphan who had captured her heart.

Dessert was waffles and Anna's princess cake of layered sponge, whipped cream, syrup, and jam wrapped in green marzipan. Then the children were all excused. For a while, the adults lingered over cups of strong brewed coffee and ginger snaps until Hanné's small cries were heard. Eva rose and settled on a chair near the fire to feed her. Lucy's heart turned over at the intimate scene. The disruption produced a general shuffle from the table; the women into the kitchen, the men to deep chairs around the fire.

By the time the dishes were done, Eva had reappeared after changing Hanné who was now swathed in a crocheted pink blanket.

"Can I have a hold now, Mummy?" Jenny begged. Eva carefully placed the baby in her arms. Beaming with delight, Jenny carried her toward Lucy. "This is my baby sister."

Without warning, she transferred Hanné into Lucy's lap. Her arms instinctively wrapped around the baby and she swallowed back a swirl of maternal emotion at the sight of the tiny snugly bundle, cherished and smothered with love as she had never been herself, a lack swiftly forgotten as she held Hanné.

"She's beautiful," Lucy said.

Jenny wrinkled her nose. "We saw her at the hospital after she was born and she looked yucky until they gave her a bath."

"Jenny, come and play," Julianna pleaded with her cousin from the playroom door.

"Okay," she called out. "You can keep Hanné," she told Lucy, sibling loyalty forgotten as she disappeared.

Lucy grinned and caught Flynn's gaze from across the room, as though he was sizing her up as motherhood material. Confused by the tender look in his eyes as she held the baby, she quickly looked away.

With school and work, the mid-week family dinner was never late. Amid kisses and hugs good night, Kristina's brood left, then Stewart with the three older children. Eva and baby Hanné would stay in the guest room a few more days.

Sitting by the fire, Flynn and Lucy finally found themselves alone with his parents, Karl half-hidden behind the thin weekly *Mundarra Standard* and Anna warming her hands around yet another well-earned cup of rich coffee.

"Thank you for dinner, Anna."

"Our pleasure, Lucy. You've always been welcome

here any time, and especially now you're home again for a while. Remember that," she insisted firmly.

"Thank you, I will."

Lucy was touched by their humble generosity and sensed that this was an opportune moment. Apprehensive, she prompted a conversation with Flynn's parents. "Do you remember much about George and Marion before they married?"

Anna raised her eyebrows in surprise and Karl, his attention captured, lowered his newspaper. Lucy hoped they thought she was being nostalgic rather than sensing the real reason for her questioning to find out more about her parents before they married and she was born. She hoped they might divulge some tiny clue, however tenuous, that led to more information.

Anna sighed. "It's a long time ago." She glanced across at her husband. "All of our generation socialized together in church groups and Saturday night pictures and dances. We were younger than George and Marion's group. They had all left school and were working already." Anna frowned, concentrating. "George came to Mundarra from elsewhere. I think he'd done some sort of business training. He was a very handsome and confident man. One could understand why Marion would be attracted. George and Marion kept company for many years before they married."

Lucy realized Anna was being tactful. It seemed their wedding had been a sudden mystery to everyone. She had a dozen questions buzzing in her head but curbed her enthusiasm to learn more and let Anna continue reminiscing.

"George was obviously going to be successful. He

bought the newsagency business soon after arriving in town and, of course, it has been in your family ever since." Anna beamed at Lucy who cringed at the deception that was necessary until more information about her real father came to hand. "I suppose the shop will be sold now?" Anna inquired innocently.

"Yes, it seems likely," Lucy tactfully replied, knowing this to be true, if not the exact circumstances. "What did my mother do after leaving school?" Lucy prompted, hoping to build on the information Anna had already shared since George and Marion had never related anything of their youth. Perhaps they preferred to forget.

"She was in the office of Wilson's Emporium. I think that's the only place she ever worked. Karl?"

He nodded. "As far as I know. She became the most senior employee. She worked there for over fifteen years until she married."

"Marion was a model employee," Anna readily divulged. "After Theo Wilson's wife, Beatrice, died, Marion sometimes accompanied him to business functions in place of one of his daughters. She was almost part of the Wilson family and involved in the business so perhaps it was logical that she held such a prominent position. Esther was your mother's good friend, of course. They went everywhere together."

"Yes, that's right." Lucy was relying on that avenue of inquiry to hopefully yield positive results.

"George was always in the background of your mother's life. He was a debonair man," Anna continued. Lucy had certainly never thought of him as such. Perhaps he had changed after the upheaval, although she felt hesitant to be charitable to the man who had, with one sweep of a signature on his will, erased her from his life. Anna's gaze softened. "Your mother was such a gentle lady. Elegant and quiet. You favor her very much in appearance and personality."

"Do I?" Lucy was touched, but more than a little amazed to hear it. She'd always thought her mother had let life happen to her whereas Lucy was inclined to go out and fight for what she wanted. Anna's comment made her wonder if she had inherited any traits from her natural father.

"You're returning to Indonesia, I expect?" Karl asked quietly.

"As soon as I can. It might be a few weeks more before I can leave though." She glanced across at Flynn. "Red tape with George's estate," she smiled weakly.

Throughout the conversation and Anna's reminiscences, Flynn had remained silent and observant. Now, he edged forward in his seat. "I don't want to keep Lucy up too late and I have an early business appointment."

Lucy took his hint and rose. "We mustn't keep your parents up either."

They said their farewells and Flynn drove Lucy home.

"You're quiet," he observed as they walked to her front door.

Lucy shrugged. "Just thinking." About so many things and her positive reactions to being with Flynn again. She sighed. "You have a wonderful family. I wish mine had been happier, but I have to look to the future now."

He moved closer, looking down at her, apparently in

no hurry to leave. "I hope you find what you're seek-ing," he whispered, giving her a soft brotherly kiss on the forehead.

She closed her eyes and savored the intimate ges-ture. She knew he meant that, like her, he still felt that old attraction but saw no future for them. "You too," she murmured, choked up with frustrating emotions and wonderful memories that refused to fade.

"The annual agricultural show is coming up next week. Think you might go?"

"Possibly." He hadn't asked her to go with him. Just checked that she might be there. After he left, she felt strangely lost and unaccountably disappointed.

Chapter Six

The telephone call from Daniel Thompson came a few days later. Within thirty minutes, Lucy was once more seated in his office.

"Good news and bad news." Daniel came straight to the point after their greetings.

"Bad first." Lucy gripped her hands together so tightly they hurt.

"The DNA results between you and George McCarthy are negative," Daniel said gently. "You're definitely not his daughter, and we've also been informed that the test results between Michael McCarthy, his mother, and George are all positive."

So, it was confirmed. Michael *was* George's son. Lucy let out a deep sigh and discovered it was just as awful hearing it a second time. She was overcome with a heavy sense of finally knowing and accepting the truth.

Daniel gave her a moment to digest the facts. "Now that proof is established," he continued, "we need to resolve the estate issues." Frankly, Lucy felt too overwhelmed to care, but she listened anyway. "Michael's lawyers have offered a settlement. I'd urge you to consider it."

"That bad, huh?" Lucy smiled wryly.

Daniel shrugged. "It's a gesture."

Lucy realized Michael was buying her off in an effort to stop the will challenge. "The illegitimate son has scruples. Who would have thought?"

Daniel tactfully ignored Lucy's anger and said, "Michael's apparently prepared to be reasonable."

"That would be a first."

"Going to court is not always the best way. Dispute resolution would be wise for everyone."

Lucy absorbed his tactful hint. "Of course. It's to Michael's advantage. Dragging out a will challenge will eat away his inheritance."

Daniel named an amount, and Lucy didn't know whether to be offended by the paltry sum or grateful that it was enough to be put to good use elsewhere and make a difference in other lives. Truthfully, she had expected nothing but a fight and the satisfaction of seeing Michael's legacy reduced, not expecting anything for herself. She estimated his offer was about ten percent of the house and business value when sold. Dirty money that she would grudgingly accept, but which she had no intention of keeping. But following Michael's overt selfishness at their only encounter, she supposed it was generous, although probably prompted on advice from his lawyer.

"At least he's acknowledged I have some moral rights. That's all I ever asked."

"I know. Payment of the money is conditional."

Lucy sighed. "On what?"

"That you immediately vacate the house."

Lucy scoffed. "What's the rush? In Mundarra, the property might not sell for months. It will just sit there, empty." She paused, adding, "How immediate?"

"Within forty-eight hours." Daniel raised his eyebrows. "Doable?"

Lucy shook her head in amazement. "Well, yes, I guess so. I've been gradually packing up what few personal possessions I know belonged to my mother. Michael is not entitled to those. There's only a few boxes. Since I travel light in my life, I'll see if I can store them somewhere."

"You're staying on a while longer then?"

Lucy nodded. "My mother lived her whole life in Mundarra. My father either lived here too at the time or had some close or regular connection with the town." She pulled a tight smile. "I just have to find out who he is. Or was."

She needed to close the McCarthy chapter of her life and move on. Focus on the new developments in her life as a result of today's DNA news. She didn't know how much she could uncover in a few weeks, but she would try.

"I wish you well, Lucy, and I'll inform Michael's Melbourne lawyers of your acceptance of all terms."

Moments, later, Lucy walked in a daze from Daniel's legal office. With all connections to George now officially severed, it felt as though her past life had never existed at all. She needed to start asking questions around town. Chatting with Anna and Karl Pedersen after dinner the other night had been interesting but not given any real clues or leads to who her father might be. Esther Wilson was her strongest link to Marion and the best prospect to yield results. As her mother's dearest friend, at the least she should know more than anyone else.

The next morning, Lucy woke early to the sound of a dull thumping outside the house. She struggled from bed and crossed to the window, drawing the curtains aside. A huge FOR SALE sign now occupied a large slice of the front garden, and an estate agent was climbing back into his station wagon with the business name emblazoned on the front door. Michael wasn't wasting time.

Lucy was a nomad. She lived out of a suitcase and certainly couldn't drag any extra possessions about with her from place to place when she moved on every few years. She sighed. It had been so nice to have the luxury of a bathroom, running water, clean surroundings. Walking paved streets, visiting decent shops. She'd been away so long and grown accustomed to living in a totally different environment, she'd forgotten how spoiled she'd been in a western civilization.

Now, she felt at loose ends, abandoned. Her life temporarily suspended in a kind of emotional limbo. No family. At least that she knew about. Yet. But she had Maya. Lucy smiled. Her little heartwarming, olive-skinned orphan treasure awaiting her return. A cuddly six-year-old soul who lavished her with unconditional affection.

Lucy had left Maya with Sari and her family, close neighbors in their village. Maya played with their children and freely darted in and out of their home, knowing she was always welcome.

Lucy had considered formal adoption, bringing Maya back to Australia and a better life, but now she had no permanent or secure home to offer the child. Until she was settled and more stable in life, she hesitated to take the next step. So she had stayed on in Indonesia to be near her, keeping the child among her own native people. The move into a European society would be a huge change for the girl and one Lucy would not take lightly.

Besides, there were so many other needy children to help. There always seemed so much more to do. She sighed, wishing now was a good time to break away, but she would have to put any plans on hold. She guessed the time would be right eventually.

Refocusing on the matter at hand, Lucy showered and dressed. Carole and Flynn were both busy working so she wouldn't ask for their help, but she could certainly seek their advice. She wondered if Carole still had that back storage room behind the salon and decided to ask. And, whatever she did, she needed a vehicle for transportation.

But, first things first. Lucy needed a roof over her head and, after breakfast, strode down to the Railway Hotel and booked herself a room for an indefinite duration. With the key safely in her pocket and a bed to sleep in, she retraced her steps, knowing she had no choice but to eat humble pie.

She forced her lagging steps toward Mundarra Motors and all those lovely vehicles in the used car yard. Through the wide front showroom windows, Lucy glimpsed Flynn on the telephone in his office. Wandering through to the reception counter area, Lucy asked to see him when he was free.

Meanwhile, she returned outdoors, scouting suitable small runabout vehicles she could use for a few weeks. She cupped her hands against the glare and peered in through the side window of a smart three-door compact hatchback.

She jumped when a male voice said close behind her, "Good choice."

Lucy turned, and the sight of Flynn took her breath away. Tailored suit, immaculately groomed. And were those Italian shoes? What was not to like? Unfortunately, she was growing accustomed to being around him again. Fate seemed to constantly be sending her to him for help. Even more disturbing was the fact that, in any kind of dilemma, she usually thought of him first.

"How do you know I'm looking?" she quipped.

"Saw the FOR SALE sign up at the house as I drove past earlier today."

"Have to move out. Reluctantly," she admitted. "Guess I have to let go of my false past sometime."

Flynn scowled. "Big changes are never easy." He looked off into the distance down the street, squinting against the bright morning sun. Maybe he was thinking of his divorce.

"Anyway," Lucy continued, "I've booked a room at the Railway."

'You didn't need to go to that expense. The guest wing is empty in my house.'

Guest wing? How big was his home? Come to think of it, she didn't even know where he lived but she was blown away by his offer. "That's very generous of you, but it's done now. Today, because I need to be on the move, I need wheels."

Flynn extended an arm, gesturing toward the main building. "Let's go in and I'll find you the keys to this car."

They started walking. "It's available?"

"For as long as you want it. They're all mechanically checked over, so it's ready to roll."

"I don't want a petrol guzzler. It should be economical to run."

"It is. And there'll be no charges involved. You can refuel it for free. I'll have a word with my service station manager."

Lucy abruptly halted in the showroom doorway as they entered. "Oh, I don't expect—"

"No arguments, Lucy. You've been through hell lately." He laid a gentle hand on her arm. "Please let me do that for you."

Overwhelmed by his generosity, she spluttered, "I don't know what to say." Who was this new person? Where was the old, more self-centered Flynn? The whole time she'd been back in Mundarra, he hadn't appeared. People were affected by the situations and changes they encountered in life. She shouldn't be so surprised by this different person standing in front of her. He'd endured an unhappy marriage and now had the responsibility of a son.

She wanted to fling her arms around him in gratitude for his offer but knew she would be out of line. "Flynn, thank you so much," she murmured in heartfelt gratitude. He seemed embarrassed by her softly spoken words of appreciation. Not many good things had happened to her lately so, when she found herself on the verge of happy tears, she held them back and turned aside, pretending to survey her surroundings. "You have a thriving business here. You must be proud."

"It's been a lot of work."

Was there an edge of regret in his voice? Had his ambition in building an empire and the time it must have taken out of his personal life caused his divorce?

"Do you want a test drive?" Flynn asked as he handed over the car keys.

"No. I noticed it's automatic. It should be fine although it's been years since I've driven anything quite so grand. My transportation is usually a motor scooter or bicycle on a crowded street or unpaved road."

Lucy didn't fully understand Flynn's frown as she thanked him and walked out to the lot to take possession of her car. She sank into its comfortable interior, maneuvered from the car yard and drove the short distance to Carole's salon along Main Street.

As she opened the shop door, a bell tinkled overhead. Her friend looked up and paused in cutting and styling a customer's hair. Carole acknowledged her and asked her to wait. Lucy browsed through women's magazines until the client left.

"Are you here for an appointment?" she asked, smiling warmly in greeting.

It was such a rare treat for Carole to be so pleasant, Lucy returned it with genuine reservations. She fingered her long straight hair, riddled with split ends. "I guess I could do with some attention but, no."

"I see you've been over talking to Flynn."

No secrets in Mundarra. "Yes, I needed transportation

to move my things. You probably noticed the house is up for sale."

"Yes. You're not messing about, are you?"

Lucy let her uninformed comment slide and hurried on. "That's why I'm here. I remember you had a storage room out back of your salon." Lucy took a deep breath and reluctantly asked her favor. "I don't suppose it's still there and that you have a corner to spare to store some boxes for me?"

"Flynn didn't have room in his big house?"

"I didn't ask." Lucy let yet another innuendo pass. "He's very busy." She knew Carole thought she and Flynn were involved. Maybe they were, to a certain extent, but Lucy was hesitant to open herself up to him for fear of being hurt again. A challenge, especially around the man who had always held a soft spot in the corner of her heart.

Sensing Carole's displeasure for whatever reason, Lucy wished she hadn't asked her for a favor. She'd had enough of rejection lately. Lucy could see her friend was miserable and wished Carole would say why so she could help. This was probably the reason they hadn't been better able to revive their old friendship in any kind of harmonious way. Funny how she had been able to ease back into easy contact with Flynn and Eva but not Carole. Time changed people in different ways.

Deciding to bow out gracefully and leave without further testing their friendship, Lucy said, "Sorry to interrupt your work, Carole." She stepped aside as the bell tinkled and two ladies entered the salon. "Don't worry. I'll find somewhere else."

She was halfway to the door, trying for a tactful exit, when Carole momentarily disregarded her elderly clients and said, "I do still have the back room. I only use it for my supplies. There's spare space in it for your things." Carole's offer was accompanied with an expression of appeal in her eyes and genuine remorse.

Lucy paused in shock and gratitude that she had reconsidered. "Are you sure?" Carole nodded. "Well, that's great. I'm happy to pay any storage rental."

Still sounding regretful, Carole quickly assured her, "That won't be necessary. The back door is always unlocked while the shop's open. Access is along the laneway beside the building."

"Thank you." Lucy smiled her appreciation of Carole's conciliatory attempt. "I really appreciate you doing this. I guess I should go now."

Carole waved an arm helplessly in the air, clearly still embarrassed by her sudden kind gesture. She smiled weakly and turned back to her customers, ushering them into chairs in front of the mirrors.

Lucy sighed as she walked out of the salon. Since her return to Mundarra, her friendship with Carole had been strangely difficult. Lucy couldn't think how she had offended her friend since returning home, but Carole had certainly been unfriendly from day one. Irony was, Carole had approached *her* the day she'd arrived.

As she climbed back into her car, Lucy decided to give it one last shot and catch up with her friend sometime for a chat, try to get her to open up and talk about whatever was really bothering her. Perhaps at that new little coffee shop she'd noticed on the north end of town. The Gumnut Café.

To keep her mind occupied and because she was under pressure to vacate the house, Lucy returned to Deacon Street and started loading boxes into her borrowed car. Because she was ducking in and out at the back of the shop, she didn't encounter Carole again on her ferrying trips to the salon.

When she had completed transferring her possessions between house and shop, Lucy took one last nostalgic stroll through the deserted lonely rooms of her old home. She wondered if Michael would be remotely interested in keeping any of the old furniture pieces as keepsakes and part of his father's heritage. Probably not. With no emotional attachment to anything, he only seemed to care about the bottom line.

Lucy actually felt an ache of sympathy and regret for her mother's obviously dismal life with George but no longer had a shred of feeling for the man himself because of his utterly contrived machinations.

Her last trip was to deliver all the canned and other food from the pantry and perishables from the refrigerator to the Christian welfare shop run by the local churches. The lady who accepted the two large boxes of goods was profusely grateful for the donation. Lucy was just glad it would go toward some local person or family in need.

Before she lost her nerve and changed her mind, Lucy drove to the north end of town, the area first settled in its early days where streets were broad and filled with large gracious homes on big blocks, surrounded by mature rambling gardens.

She pushed open the rusted ornamental iron gate of Esther Wilson's house. With sadness, her eyes took in the overgrown garden where rose bushes struggled through weeds into valiant full bloom. She trod the brick-paved footpath up to the gracious old weatherboard home fully circled by deep verandas.

She rapped the lion head knocker in the center of the paneled front door, noting the tarnished brass nameplate ROSELEIGH alongside. Soon, footsteps sounded from inside and the door slowly opened.

Essie's smooth complexion paled at the sight of her visitor as though she'd seen a ghost. Her thick white hair was brushed neatly off her face and she wore a pretty cotton print dress with a string of pearls.

"Lucy." Her name was barely a whisper on the slight woman's lips.

"Hello, Essie." Lucy smiled, trying to stifle her trepidation but not her hope. "It's lovely to see you again."

"Yes." Essie's voice quavered. "We didn't get a chance to chat at George's funeral."

Lucy now realized the older woman had made herself noticeably scarce after the service and hadn't attended the tea gathering in the church hall. Odd, particularly since throughout childhood Lucy clearly recalled regular visits between Essie and Marion in each other's homes. The two women had been as close as sisters.

"Do you have time for a quick chat?"

Essie looked positively terrified but, after a moment's pause, she said, "Of course, my dear."

Although polite and welcoming, she was clearly disturbed over Lucy's visit. Perhaps it was just the wariness of an elderly lady living alone or maybe she preferred to be forewarned and organized. Whatever the reason, Essie was unenthusiastic about her arrival. Lucy was starting to feel a trend of rejection since her return to town.

Recovering, Essie stepped aside and ushered Lucy into a dim sitting room crammed with dark, heavy furniture. "I don't get many visitors," Essie murmured apologetically as she moved to the window, raising blinds behind lace curtains and velvet drapes. Lucy ran a concerned glance over layers of dust the daylight revealed. "I'll just go and boil the kettle for a pot of tea." She hovered nervously in the doorway, as though about to say something, before disappearing.

She soon returned with a tray. The floral cups, saucers, and teapot were Royal Albert, Lucy knew, because her mother had also appreciated and collected fine china. Marion's pieces were safely boxed away where Michael McCarthy could never get his hands on them.

The older woman sat opposite, hands folded in her lap and patiently waited.

"How have you been?" Lucy struggled to start a conversation.

"I can't complain about a few aches and pains at my age." Essie gave a faint polite smile, her posture tense and expectant.

Not wanting to waste any more time than necessary and strain any emotions, Lucy decided directness was the best approach. "Essie, something has arisen, and I need your help." Because she had been her mother's best friend, Lucy wanted her to know the latest developments in her life, so she detailed everything she had recently learned about George's betrayal, his will, and Michael.

Clutching the pearls at her throat and shaking her head, Essie muttered, "Marion was too good for him."

Essie didn't seem particularly surprised by the revelations Lucy had just shared, and that reaction alone lifted her spirits. "Then why did they marry?" Lucy watched her closely.

Distress crossed Essie's averted face. "Sometimes we make wrong choices, my dear."

"It doesn't matter now. He's not my father anyway. And that's why I'm here." Lucy noticed Essie's hand grip the side of her chair. The woman's discomfort gave her hope. "You were close to my mother. Do you have any idea who my natural father might be?"

"My memory is not what it used to be," she murmured after an awkward silence.

"Did my mother ever say or hint anything to you?"

Essie cast her a pleading glance. "It's all so long ago . . ."

She was deliberately stalling! Was the mysterious past too painful to recall and voice or had it been buried for so long it was just difficult to raise again?

"Essie, was my mother seeing another man? Was there someone else in her life?" Lucy paused, adding gently, "Someone only *you* might know about?"

"Marion was an attractive and popular young woman."

Lucy took a deep breath for patience over Essie's obvious evasion and sipped her tea. "That's strange. Others have mentioned that mother was really only keeping company with George."

"Oh, she was much in demand at all the social events. She didn't only dance with George."

"I'm sure she didn't."

Although Essie was persistently stubborn, Lucy's frustration was blitzed by her growing excitement. The other woman knew something she was sure but, for now, she didn't press. She would give her time to think it over and visit again. Not wanting to reveal that Essie hadn't fooled her, Lucy pulled out one last tactic.

She heaved a long theatrical sigh. "I'm so disappointed. I was convinced you must remember something. Being so close to my mother, I was hoping she might have confided in you and I might learn something before I leave."

Essie's eyes widened in alarm. "Leaving? When? You're not staying for a while?"

"I have no reason now, do I? My family was a sham and I no longer have a home here." She needed Essie to believe she would never return so that, in alarm, she might be prepared to share the truth about her mother that Lucy was convinced she knew.

"Oh. Of course." Essie's agitation told Lucy she wanted to say more, but didn't.

Lucy rose to leave, having planted the seed and hoping it bore fruit. She would be devastated if Essie kept any secrets to herself.

"If you remember anything at all . . ." She pressed Essie's hand at the door and flashed an encouraging smile but received only a fearful stare in return.

As Lucy strode away from Roseleigh and back to the car, she prayed she had penetrated Essie's resistance enough to unlock whatever had existed in the past. Now she could only wait.

Chapter Seven

Flynn tossed his car keys onto the central island bench of his huge country-style kitchen with its wide picture windows, their normal view across the garden now cloaked in darkness. It was late and he was bushed. He'd spent a couple of hours since closing up his dealership for the day talking to residents of the Lakeside retirement village, hoping, for Lucy's sake, someone would remember something about her mother.

Unfortunately, he'd had no luck. Few recalled anything of Marion Greenwood's youth before she married George McCarthy. Flynn wondered how he could break the disappointing news to Lucy. She was pinning such hopes on finding out who her father was, and he hated to dash them. Having her back in town, even temporarily, had given his life meaning again, built up hope that he knew he was foolish to chase.

He rubbed a hand over his weary face and, opening the refrigerator door, unenthusiastically eyed the lovely evening meal his housekeeper, Mabel Taylor, had prepared and left for him.

As his dinner rotated in the microwave, the telephone rang and he sighed. Being a pillar of the community was all well and good, but it ate into his personal life. The irony wasn't lost on him. These days, he didn't have a personal life.

He reached for the wall phone before the machine picked it up. "Pedersen," he snapped, hoping this wouldn't take long.

"Flynn. Darling."

The two words, especially the last one of phoney endearment, rang alarm bells in his brain. The last thing he felt like at the moment was another confrontation with his ex-wife.

"Sandy." He tried to inject a smile into his voice. He shunned pleasantries, trusting she would get to the point of her call. She only phoned when she wanted something. Besides, he was starving.

In hindsight, he now realized his marriage had been on the rebound after Lucy had fled from Mundarra while she had the chance. He didn't blame her; she'd had a fire in her belly to help unfortunate kids. In his heart, he wasn't sure he'd ever really forgiven her for so readily deserting him for strangers. He'd seen a different woman since her return, and his harsh opinion of former times had softened.

Feeling guilty, he'd compensated for his hasty marriage by plowing himself into building up a successful business to give his social shopaholic wife and cherished son security and a good lifestyle. Granted, it had sucked up most of his time, but he'd done it for his family. Sandy was high-maintenance and, for a while, he'd been proud to have her by his side. Until the first of many times she'd strayed. He'd repeatedly forgiven her until their marriage was an empty mess and Sandy only stayed with him for the money. That was never a problem for Flynn. He seemed to have a Midas touch and simply went out and made more.

Deep in thought, Flynn had tuned out, but Sandy's conversation finally pierced his consciousness and caught his attention.

"So Marcus wants our holiday on Lizard Island up on the reef to be just the two of us. Alone."

Who was Marcus, Flynn scowled as Sandy chattered on, trying to remember if she'd ever mentioned him before? She had a new admirer every week. This latest one better shape up. Whoever he was, Flynn only hoped the man was a decent role model around his son. It was bad enough that each parent lived on opposite sides of the country.

"So you can see the dilemma that creates," Sandy whined. "Mother is away in Europe, and you know I don't have any other family I can rely on. Except you." She sounded hopeful. "A whole week would give you time to bond with little Joshie."

Little? Their son was halfway through primary school already. Sandy still treated him like a baby. Flynn massaged the back of his neck as Sandy prattled on. If he had it right, she was asking him to have their son for a week because she wanted to swan off to a tropical island with her newest boyfriend.

No problem. He'd take any opportunity to spend time with Joshua outside his legal access. He loved being a father and hated that his son lived across the Nullarbor in Perth, thousands of kilometers away. Probably deliberately engineered by Sandy, Flynn suspected. However, Joshua's visit couldn't have come at a busier time for him. He had an important meeting with fuel executives who were flying down especially from Sydney to discuss his next major project.

At a pinch, he could occasionally rely on his housekeeper. His mind searched about for how he could entertain a lively eight-year-old for a week. At least the local agricultural show would be on while Josh was here. Between fun rides and fairy floss, that should keep him happy for a day. Businesses closed for the day so he would have some free time.

Another idea hit him and he wondered if he dared.

He and Sandy finalized details and flight times for Josh's arrival in Melbourne, then hung up. As Flynn took his heated meal into his office to work out the finer details of the upcoming business deal while he ate, his brain scrambled about for solutions to reschedule his week, slotting in an eight-hour round trip down to Melbourne to pick up his son from the airport.

He looked forward to seeing Josh again. He only saw him a few times a year and the boy was growing fast. He knew he missed out on a lot and their limited visits were inadequate to build a strong relationship, but Sandy had custody and he had restricted access. Very restricted. Thanks to Sandy's expensive predatory lawyer who he was convinced had been hired only to hurt Flynn as much as possible.

Since Sandy had been unfaithful and he'd been the one filing for divorce, her vindictive behavior had hurt like hell at the time, especially with an innocent child involved. But he'd forced himself to move on emotionally, determined to financially support his grown son to the highest degree possible. Everything he achieved was for his son and he worked hard to make it happen.

The constant nagging thought sitting on his shoulders that he had so far been unable to shake off was the fact that he must have been a lousy husband for Sandy to stray. Which pushed him in his personal commitment to being a better father. Whenever he had the chance.

His next objective was to contact Lucy and put forward the proposition he had in mind.

Lucy left her borrowed car parked at the hotel and wandered through town toward the lake. Now that she had vacated the house and George's estate settlement was finalized, she was only marking time the best she could and wait for developments on her real father's identity. She hated being inactive. She needed to be busy, challenged.

She should think of her remaining time in Mundarra more positively as the holiday she hadn't taken in years. She'd briefly considered driving down to Melbourne for a few days but decided against it, afraid Essie might try to contact her again and she'd miss the call. She hadn't heard from Flynn in recent days, but she'd been busy packing up and moving out of Deacon Street. He was obviously tied up with business.

Although she might deny it, she enjoyed seeing Flynn again. Since the friction of their first meetings after she arrived back in town, there had seemed less tension between them the last few times they'd met. Conversation became easier, despite their reserve with each other. The knowledge frightened her because they'd both cared deeply for each other. Once. And had both been hurt by disappointment when they realized they needed to go their separate ways. Those same old feelings and doubts hadn't disappeared when she was around him again. He still seemed the same consummate and successful businessman but perhaps without quite so much the same manic drive.

Flynn had offered to interview some elderly citizens at Lakeside about her mother and she longed to hear if he'd discovered anything. Lucy prayed he had because then she wouldn't have to pin all her hopes on Essie Wilson and have her expectations crushed if her hunch about her mother's good friend proved false. Waiting was tough.

Truthfully, Lucy would not know where to turn next in the search for her father if that avenue came to nothing. All she could hope for was that some small snippet of information emerged, leading *somewhere*.

Reaching the lake, Lucy strolled along its shores until fate or coincidence brought her to the wooden bench that backed up against a weeping willow, letting the occupant look out across the rippling waters and watch the ducks and swans paddling among the reeds at its edges.

Lucy swept aside the lacy drooping branches that with every passing year seemed to hang farther over the seat, partly shrouding it from view, creating a peaceful sanctuary for contemplation. She'd often come here when she was growing up to escape the tension at home.

The late afternoon sun reflected diamonds of sparkling light off the lake's surface. Lucy raised a hand to shield the glare, so she didn't immediately recognize the person approaching until a shadow fell across her line of vision.

"Flynn." Lucy was surprised to see him away from his business in the middle of a working day.

He indicated the bench. "May I?"

"Sure." Lucy shuffled across as he sat beside her and stretched an arm along the back of the seat.

Her previous calm deserted her to see him looking dashing in a business suit and tie, shoes highly polished. The old sense of inadequacy returned because, due to the milder spring weather of late, she was dressed down, as usual, in a T-shirt and long cotton sarong, one of many she had rolled up and stuffed into her suitcase for the sudden trip home. Besides shorts, tank tops, and sandals, they comprised her daily attire overseas. Everyone else wore them for comfort in the heat, and she had also adopted the mode of dress because it helped her blend in.

Lucy always felt she never quite measured up to Flynn's impeccable standards. He was so ambitious, whereas her life had coasted along a simpler road. Yet she respected him greatly for his achievements and was beginning also to feel a warmth and caring for him too.

"I'm surprised you found me," she remarked, smiling her pleasure.

"This is Mundarra, Lucy." He flashed her an easy devastating grin. "I went to your old house and found it locked up. Your former neighbor Mrs. Dawson just happened to be hovering at the front fence. She must have thought I was trying to break in because she came rushing over. It gave her great pleasure to tell me you had vacated and moved into the Railway already."

Lucy shrugged. "No point in delaying the inevitable.

Besides, I didn't really have much choice." No need to indulge in self-pity and how lost she'd felt, like a marble rattling around in an empty jar. "Why were you looking for me?"

Flynn studied his hands, then explained his lack of success in speaking to the Lakeside residents, ending with an apology.

Lucy sighed. "Well, it's certainly a disappointment but thanks for trying. However," her voice brightened, "all is not lost. I've spoken to Essie Wilson, and I'm convinced she knows something but won't say." She quickly related the gist of her conversation with her mother's closest friend.

Flynn raised his eyebrows with interest. "Sounds promising."

"It is." Lucy found it hard to contain her optimism talking about it again. "So I'm trying to keep myself busy doing nothing for a few days and hope my visit brings developments sooner rather than later. So in the meantime, I've offered to help Carole in her salon for a few hours most days in repayment for allowing me to store all my boxes in the back of her shop."

"It's one way of catching up with all the local gossip, I suppose," he teased.

Lucy found she rather enjoyed this lighter side to Flynn. "It's certainly interesting hearing their grizzles about the petty things in their lives. All the things they take for granted, but I guess they can't understand their comfort if they haven't traveled to poorer countries to compare."

"No, they haven't experienced what you have," he observed quietly.

She smiled, pleased he understood. He hadn't once. When he suddenly grew quiet, she glanced at him and caught him smiling at her. "What?"

"Nothing." After a pause, he asked, "How do you fill in the rest of your day?"

"With difficulty," she admitted wryly. "Go for walks. E-mail Maya from the library's Internet connection."

Flynn nodded and hesitated again. "I may have a solution to your problem. At least for a day or two." He related the details of Sandy's telephone call and request.

Lucy was privately elated that Flynn was asking her to help out and trusted her in caring for his son. "I'm flattered you thought of me, and I'd be delighted to mind Joshua." She could never turn her back on any child or refuse his or her needs.

"I can feel a *but* coming on."

He looked wounded, and Lucy hadn't even explained her position yet. Did he have so little faith in her and honestly believe she would let him down? Perhaps he expected a repeat of her abandonment once before all those years ago.

Lucy took a deep breath and voiced the concerns on her mind. "As far as I can see with your service station and car dealership, you get the majority of automotive business in town. You're successful. You've made it. I seem to remember that was always your goal, and I congratulate you for achieving it." She paused. "You're the boss. You employ a large staff, so you should be able to delegate, take time off. Have you considered doing that while Joshua is here with you?"

"Of course." His cool gaze and grinding jaw revealed his displeasure at her challenging outburst.

"So?"

"I won't be free all the time Josh is here. I'd appreci-ate your help."

Lucy knew it must have been difficult for him to ask. But why her? "What about your housekeeper, Mabel?"

"She's only part time and has a big family of her own, but if you're free and you have some spare time . . ." he trailed off and shrugged.

Lucy suspected most females would willingly do the same for him given the opportunity. Especially with the whispers she'd heard in the salon of Sandy Pedersen's infidelity. While there were always two sides to every story, it seemed his ex-wife must shoulder a good por-tion of the blame. Marriage sure was a lottery, Lucy mused. Which is why she'd backed away from it. It wasn't totally out of the question for her future but if, and when, she ever got married, it would be to the right bloke, at the right time, and for all the right reasons.

"What about Karl and Anna?" she queried, refocusing.

"They have their hands full with Eva's new baby and minding all their other grandchildren."

"They seem devoted grandparents to me and they hardly ever see Joshua. It would be a thrill for them to have him."

"They will. For one day." He paused. "Can you help me out or not?" he asked curtly, clearly offended by her interrogation.

"Of course I will. I look forward to meeting your son."

"Thank you." His mood was a combination of grati-tude and irritation. "I *am* aware of my responsibilities as a father." He rose from the bench to angrily pace back and forth in front of her. "I'm not being neglectful. I hardly ever have the chance to see him. I wouldn't ask if it wasn't important. Day after tomorrow, I have a crucial meeting about business expansion."

"Expanding?" Lucy gasped, having a light bulb moment about his real reason for seeking her help. "You're not big enough already?" Dismayed, she couldn't resist the taunt.

"It's about buying into a national franchise. It's too good an opportunity not to explore. These people are movers and shakers, Lucy. They're flying in especially from Sydney."

"I don't care if it's a deputation from OPEC in Vienna," Lucy scoffed in exasperation. "I know what it's like to be a neglected child. You don't put everything else before family. Sometimes sacrifices have to be made."

"In this case, I have no choice."

"There's always a choice," Lucy argued. "Your parents are ideal role models. Haven't you learned anything from them?"

"I'm aware of my warm and supportive family and also that not every child has one." He sent her a meaningful and compassionate glance. "I more than adequately provide for my wife and son. I may have failed the marriage, but I can sure as hell make sure they're covered financially."

Lucy gazed in awe at Flynn's defensive stance and simmering anger. "Is that how you feel?" she whispered, appalled at his admission. "That you're a failure? Are you trying to make up for it with money?"

When he didn't answer, she suspected she'd dug to the truth of his continued drive to expand. He'd exceeded her expectations since her return by helping her cope and being around when she had needed someone so desperately in the first days after her arrival. Being asked to mind Joshua was a golden opportunity to repay that kindness. Sensitive about her own childhood, she just hated to think Flynn would put his son second but, given his logical explanations, perhaps she'd read him wrong. That seemed to be happening a lot lately.

Lucy folded her arms and said quietly. "Just let me know when and where you need me. I'll be there."

A shadow of relief crossed Flynn's face and dissolved the tension. "Thank you."

"You came to my rescue recently. It's the least I can do."

"I'm driving down to Melbourne to pick up Josh from the airport about midday. My meeting is the day after tomorrow."

"Sure. I'll tell Carole I'm unavailable that day. Do you have any preference for how you'd like me to entertain him?"

Flynn shrugged. "Just be around for him."

Lucy grinned. "Sounds a bit boring for an active eight-year-old. I'm sure we can do way better than that." She already had some ideas in mind. "Since I can hardly amuse him at the pub, you'd better tell me where you live."

"Two miles out the Lake Road. Turn left at the intersection. The house driveway becomes gravel and runs right off the road. Just go straight on through the entrance. Gate's always open."

Chapter Eight

Two days later, when Lucy saw the stone pillars on either side of the gateway pointing toward the long gum-lined road leading up to the house, she gaped as she drove through. Gates. These weren't just gates, they were a statement. As if that wasn't impressive enough, at the end there was a circular lawn and graveled driveway sweeping elegantly before an astonishing three-winged country house. Its warm sandstone glowed with welcome in the morning sun. Lucy's first thought was that Flynn lived here alone in this grand place. But then, of course he would have built it for Sandy and Joshua. In happier times.

Flynn's four-wheel drive was parked out in front. As she alighted from her borrowed car, the double front doors opened to reveal a man and a boy. A sheltie dashed out from inside and ran up to greet her, tail wagging.

"Hello, boy." She rubbed his head.

"*Lady*, sit." At the sound of the firm male voice, the beautiful dog instantly obeyed.

When she glanced up, Lucy caught her breath. Standing side by side, Joshua was a smaller version of his father, equally handsome in his own youthful way and, if she was not mistaken, equally reserved. In a few years, he would dazzle teenage girls. The thought made Lucy nostalgic.

"Hi," she said tentatively, smiling. "I hope I'm not late."

"No," Flynn said easily. "We've been waiting for you." Although there was hardly any need for introductions, he turned to his son and draped an arm around his shoulders. "Joshua, this is Lucy—" He abruptly stopped. She was sure he'd been about to say her surname, but he simply finished with, "she'll be spending some time with you today while I'm away."

The boy politely extended a hand. "How do you do, Lucy."

Lucy smiled to herself at his gentlemanly formality. He was either strictly raised or spent much of his time around adults. There was an air of restrained energy about him. Again, she couldn't help comparing him to his father. "Pleased to meet you, Joshua." She accepted his small warm hand. "I can promise you, we're going to have a great day together."

When Flynn gestured them forward to the house, Lucy's awe over the striking exterior turned to jaw-dropping amazement at the luxury and comfort inside. The wide, tiled entry hall was filled with huge tubs of lush plants and flooded with light from the overhead, domed skylight and a wall of French windows at the other end. They walked straight through toward them, turning into a huge sunny kitchen and dining area in gleaming white with polished timber floors and bench tops and a central island bench. More French doors drew her eyes to the paved patio and leafy garden view beyond. The words classy and peaceful drifted into Lucy's mind.

"This is a cook's dream." She smiled, asking mischievously, "Do you use it much?"

Joshua wrinkled his nose and innocently revealed, "Mabel does. She leaves our meals in the refrigerator, and we heat them in the microwave."

Convenient for two lost males perhaps but rather sad when put into its wider perspective. This kitchen was aching to be filled with people and laughter, cooking aromas drifting out from the oven, fingers being sneakily dipped into bowls of baking mixture. Lucy couldn't help comparing all this to Flynn's simple and warm family home around the lake. A house needed to be filled with people to make it into a home, and this one was certainly crying out for such treatment. Lucy felt a deep compassion for Flynn, living in such comfortable surroundings alone, and she only now began to understand what his life was like.

"How was your plane trip?" she addressed his son.

"I've done it before," he said indifferently, like a seasoned traveler. "Sometimes with my mother and sometimes on my own."

"You're very lucky. Not all children have the chance."

At Joshua's proud insistence, Lucy patiently allowed him to lead her on a guided tour of the rest of the house. It was all as equally stunning and plush, and all of it with Lady trotting along around them.

"Quite a palace for a bachelor," Lucy observed lightly to Flynn, not intending any offense.

"It was built as a family home. It might be again one day." He seemed self-conscious and edgy to leave. She sent him a quick appealing glance of apology.

By this time, Joshua seemed more at ease with Lucy, for which she was grateful.

As they waved his father off from the front door, Lucy asked Joshua, "What kind of things do you like to do."

"Ride my bike."

Which he did at great speed up and down the long length of the driveway while the chocolate cake they'd baked was cooling and Lucy cleaned up in the kitchen. Sitting on a high stool at the kitchen island, Joshua's feet dangled high above the lower rung while they'd taken turns adding ingredients to the mixture and giving it a stir. As his confidence grew in her company, he opened up and chatted more, his blue eyes sparkling, so reminiscent of his father. Lucy discovered he had a quiet teasing personality, which she resolved to foster. For her money, she considered him far too serious for a boy his age and was determined to lighten his mood. At least for a day.

"Let's shoot hoops in my basketball ring out back."

Which they did together after the cake was smothered with thick frosting and they'd each indulged in a generous wedge. Despite being shorter, Joshua's obvious skill and practice were a match for Lucy as they laughed and jostled their way with friendly rivalry to see who could outdo the other in shooting goals. Joshua won.

Before lunch, Lucy browsed through the bookshelves in his room while he played a computer game on his personal laptop. Because he took all this for granted but seemed unaffected by it, Lucy suggested he log onto her MySpace page on the Internet where she kept a photograph of Maya.

"She has really brown skin." He glanced up at Lucy, standing beside him. "She doesn't look like you. Is she your daughter?"

"No, but I've cared for her since she was orphaned a few years ago, so she's become my foster child."

"Are you married?"

"No."

"Why not?"

Lucy laughed. "Because I'm too busy looking after children I guess."

"You'll get married one day, won't you? Everyone does."

"Married?" A challenging question to which, despite all her reservations, the deep down honest answer was, "Yes, I hope to one day. I'd love children of my own." She was surprised by her admission. Her previous firm denials, it seemed, were up for review. It was the myth of the unattainable idyllic family that gave her pause for thought and kept her wary.

"My Dad's nice, but he's very busy. He says he doesn't have time for marriage again." He went silent for a moment, then added, with seeming reluctance, "He and my mother got divorced."

"Yes, I know. And I'm sorry." Lucy laid a hand gently on his shoulder. "It must have been sad for you all."

"Not my Mum. She has lots of men who want to be her husband again. She likes to dress up and go out."

"Sounds like fun."

Joshua turned brooding. "It is for her, but I have to stay at home with babysitters."

"Oh dear," Lucy sighed, trying to lighten his mood. "Do you mean like me?"

He nodded but brightened. "But you're different. The others just send me off to watch television or play games on my computer. You're fun."

"Well, let's have some more then, shall we? What do you say to a ride into town and a visit to the bakery for a pie with tomato sauce and a vanilla slice for lunch?'

Joshua beamed. "Cool."

Lucy had eaten rice and Asian food for so long she was equally looking forward to the small meat pie in pastry with ketchup and the lovely thick square of vanilla custard sandwiched between flaky pastry and iced.

The way to a man's heart, she mused, feeling a glowing warmth as the boy slipped his hand briefly into hers on the walk out to her car. They sped back into town, joined the long line of customers, ordered their lunch from among the selection of tantalizing aromas, then took their white paper bags of food down to the lake and sat on Lucy's favorite bench to eat it, taking their time, enjoying every last crumb.

The sun had come out with strength, drenching the golden day in early spring warmth. A quarter of the way farther around the lake was an adventure playground. After they had eaten, Joshua dragged Lucy to her feet, begging her to take him around there.

"You run on ahead," she chuckled. "I'm still having trouble moving after all that lunch."

The boy needed no urging and raced off excitedly, weaving his way along the footpath, scaring ducks who squawked and flapped away from the water's edge as he ran.

Lucy sat on a seat to one side of the playground, watching Joshua try everything in the adventure playground. Twice. He yahooed every time she pushed him off the flying fox then dared her to try it too. She did and had a ball. She'd never allowed herself this much time and relaxation to simply enjoy life. It pleased her to discover Joshua was as much therapy for her as she was company for him. They bounced off each other. They connected. And, by later afternoon, she was feeling a truly sublime sense of inner peace and uncomplicated happiness as they drove back to the homestead together.

They had only been back ten minutes when Flynn telephoned. "I've been trying to get you. Where have you been?" He sounded anxious.

"Out."

"Where?"

"I'll let Joshua tell you when you get home." Lucy assured him they were having a wonderful day and not to feel under any pressure to hurry back. "How's your meeting going?"

"Encouraging," he said curtly before hanging up.

Lucy knew Flynn's efforts probably signaled some wonderful business deal and coup but, on the other hand, she couldn't help feeling it would mean even less time for anything else but work.

Later, Joshua settled down to watch one of the Harry Potter movies on DVD from a vast collection while Lucy decided what to cook for dinner. She ignored Mabel's neatly labeled packaged meals and raided the refrigerator, freezer, and pantry.

Lucy set the small leg of lamb in a roasting pan and sprinkled over a handful of chopped rosemary picked fresh from the garden. By six, its savory aroma filtered through the house. She peeled potatoes and pumpkin, adding them to the pan. She kept checking the kitchen clock. Flynn was very late. Joshua occasionally hovered then returned to the adjoining living area to watch television, looking lost, obviously waiting for his father to return.

When vehicle headlights streamed down the driveway, Joshua was out the door to greet his father. Hanging close and babbling with excitement about his day, Lucy heard snippets of *Lucy this* and *Lucy that* as Joshua accompanied Flynn into the kitchen. He looked weary and slid a finger into the neck of his crisp white shirt to loosen his tie.

"How was your day?" Lucy asked brightly.

"Long."

He looked so utterly beat, Lucy hoped all his efforts proved worthwhile. She wasn't confident enough or involved in his life enough to pry and ask. She figured if he felt like talking, he would.

"I've taken the liberty of cooking dinner," she responded to his sweeping glance over the chaos in the kitchen.

"Smells good."

"Can Lucy stay with us to eat it?" Joshua asked.

He ruffled his son's head and glanced across at her. "I certainly hope so. She's gone to all the trouble of cooking for us, the least she can do is stay to eat it, hey, Champ?"

Joshua grinned and darted back into the lounge.

"Thank you," Lucy said softly. "I accept, but I won't stay long. You and Joshua will want some time together."

"Stay as long as you like. It's nice having you around," he murmured. His steady gaze settled on her for a moment before he added, "If I have time, I'm going to take a hot shower. Be back in fifteen?"

Lucy nodded. "I'll get Joshua to set the table while I make the gravy."

She showed Joshua how to place the cutlery and set out glasses, and gently scolded him when he picked at the crispy edges of the meat as Lucy carved it.

"My mum never cooks," Joshua confided.

Lucy was amazed to hear it, but the kitchen wasn't every woman's forte. "What do you do for meals, then?"

"Her friends take us out or we get takeaways. I love meat."

"Obviously," she teased as he sneaked another warm piece of the tender, sliced lamb.

They were chuckling when Flynn emerged again, changed into cord jeans and a light knit jumper with the sleeves pushed up to his elbows. He looked casual and huggable. Lucy felt a nostalgic ache of pleasure at the sight of him and foolishly wished that she had the courage to let him into her heart and life. She put on a brave front all through serving and eating dinner because for so long she hadn't thought that being part of a family of her own was what she wanted. Since returning to Mundarra, though, she was quickly changing her mind.

Joshua constantly chattered about their day together until he started yawning and growing quiet.

"Teeth and bed, Champ," Flynn hinted.

Joshua pulled a disapproving mouth. "Can I see Lucy again?"

Startled by his request, she quickly reassured him, "Yes, of course. I'll write my e-mail on a piece of paper and leave it on the kitchen bench, okay?"

He gave a tired smile and nodded.

"And you can contact me any time while I'm still here." Joshua knew she was returning to Indonesia since she had briefly mentioned it during the afternoon while looking at Maya's photo and they had promised to keep in touch. He seemed interested and she didn't see it could cause any harm.

"What do you say to Lucy?" Flynn prompted.

His piercing blue gaze sparkled across the table at her, and Joshua said shyly, "I had the best day. Thanks."

"You're pretty cool company yourself."

As father and son walked away, she heard Joshua ask, "Can Lucy come to the show with us, Dad?"

Flynn murmured something she didn't catch as she rose from the table and began clearing away the dishes, chuffed but embarrassed by Joshua's request. Fifteen minutes later, Flynn quietly sauntered back into the kitchen just as she finished stacking the dishwasher and wiping down the benches. The leftover sliced meat she piled onto a plate under plastic wrap in the refrigerator.

They stared at each other for a moment before he said, "You've won a heart there. Josh couldn't stop talking about you. And the dinner," he paused, "was above and beyond. Thank you."

"My pleasure. Beats returning to an uninviting hotel room."

They were awkward with each other a moment longer

until Lucy mumbled, "I should be getting back into town."

"To that uninviting room?" he teased and headed for the elegant stainless steel espresso machine. "The least I can do is make you a coffee after all your efforts on our behalf today."

Lucy normally drank tea but didn't have the heart to tell him. "All right. Sounds heavenly." She sauntered into the lounge, nestling into the plush softness of a long leather sofa, and was rubbing her arms through the light material of her long sleeved shirt against the early evening chill when he brought in her hot drink.

"You're cold." He scowled, moving across to the hearth and setting light to a small fire already set.

As the flames flickered into life and licked around the logs in a warming glow and she sipped her delicious brewed coffee, Lucy filled with a treacherous contentment.

She might not have a family, but she had moments like these that would become precious memories. No matter how itinerant her lifestyle, she could take them with her wherever she went and never forget them.

Mesmerized by the fire and captivated by what might have been, she wistfully stared into the fire. "Do you remember when we were kids all swimming in the lake on summer holidays?"

Flynn nodded. "Sure do. Every kid in town headed for the water in the heat."

"The cloudy water and squishy sand between your toes on the bottom before they built the new pool complex with that beautiful clear blue water."

"Do you remember the old German man, Mr. Meyer,

who lived in a shack on the edge of town and kept to himself?"

Lucy brightened, remembering. "Yes! After he died, the block was neglected, and we were terrified to go near it. Year by year the hut crumbled, grass was a meter high—"

"And Miss Whitehall in sixth grade. She was a dragon."

Lucy chuckled and shrugged. "Maybe she was unhappy. I don't think anyone liked her. You erased a whole lesson of hers from the blackboard once when she left the classroom," she charged him affably.

"She never found out who did it." Flynn seemed proud of the achievement.

"She was furious. She'd written it out so carefully in her beautiful writing." Lucy eyed him playfully. "I never thought of you as being rebellious."

They looked at each other and burst into laughter. When they sobered, Lucy was compelled to prompt, "I never could fathom why you did that. It was so unlike you."

Flynn didn't immediately answer, but his eyes filled with compassion. "Because she'd been giving you a hard time."

Amazed at his level of perception and concern way back then, Lucy easily recalled the spinsterish victimization. "I did seem to be singled out for criticism there for a while, didn't I?"

"Wrongly. All the kids noticed. You were an A student," he scowled, clearly annoyed. "She had no reason."

"Seems you're my protector again lately, coming to my rescue."

"Happy to oblige."

Lucy sighed and stretched. Their eyes met in mutual understanding. Like it or not, there was an attraction building between them, and it scared the hell out of her. She gave herself a mental shake. This could not be happening, yet it was so strong, virtually impossible to ignore or resist.

For a while, neither made a move. They sipped their coffee and stared into the fire. Just sat together afraid to touch alongside each other on the sofa. Then Flynn gently raised her hand and kissed it fondly, capturing her attention. He gently brushed the hair back off her face and kissed her neck and earlobe. Lucy closed her eyes and sighed. Then he trailed kisses over her cheek and chin, seeking her mouth. She turned toward him, alarmed to see such adoration in those blue eyes. She marveled how she could have let this man in under her radar again, but they were certainly both different this time around. More mellow, less inclined to argue. Dissension had been a major cause of their teenage split.

"Flynn—"

"Don't think," he whispered. "Let's just enjoy the moment, hmm?"

"I don't know if I can."

He slid an arm around her shoulder, drew her close. "Let's try, shall we?"

So they did and, snuggled protectively against him, she responded, her whole body coming alive as never before. At this rate she would never make it home.

"You kissed me back," he teased.

"You're a hard man to resist, Flynn Pedersen. I can't believe this is happening again," she sighed.

Flynn shrugged and grinned. "Just go with the flow. I am."

Wise words? Maybe. Here and now, what else could she do? When he looked down at her it seemed the most natural thing in the world that they should kiss, again. He slid a hand behind her neck and threaded his fingers into her mass of thick hair, repeating and lingering over the experience.

"Pretty damn good, huh?" Lucy nodded, but her head buzzed with warning. As if reading her confusion, Flynn murmured, "Don't think. Just feel."

Feeling languid and cherished by a man who made no secret of his attraction and unable to control her own, they kissed again for a wonderfully long while. She didn't even try to pull away. Her mind and body had long since surrendered to the magic of learning this man all over again and questioning how wise it was to do so. Even though she knew their future was headed for big trouble.

After they had settled together for a while in silence, coffee cups long since abandoned on a side table, Flynn asked casually, "Do you think you'll ever come back?"

Lucy was surprised by the abrupt question but knew exactly what he meant. Would she ever return to Mundarra to stay. She took a moment to collect her thoughts before she posed, "It's always a possibility but, right now, I have no reason to, do I?"

She glanced at him. His face was a blank mask but his blue eyes washed softly over her. Her heart pounded with adrenalin hoping he might declare his true feelings, but he didn't. She thought of all the words she could say to him, wanted to say to him but dared not. To admit to still having feelings for Flynn after all these years was going to cause one giant headache. She just knew it. Clearly, he felt the same way but appeared hesitant to reveal it. Since she'd arrived back in town, the chemistry between them had been so instant and strong, it had caught her off guard so that, for Lucy, their renewed romance made her feel breathless and rushed.

All future hurdles had slipped to the back of her mind when, to her surprise, he'd raised the issue she had heard voiced earlier. "Josh is spending the day with his grandparents tomorrow, but the day after, the town will be shut down for the annual show. Have you thought any more about it?"

"To be honest, I haven't decided."

"Josh would love you to come."

Not exactly how she would have preferred it phrased. "What about you?" she teased in challenge.

"I've just kissed you to distraction. You know *my* feelings. Of course I want you along."

Lucy filled with frustration, totally confused. If she agreed to Flynn's invitation, it meant spending even more time together. On the one hand, Lucy didn't want to encourage his attraction, yet on the other, she couldn't deny loving his company and the prospect of being with Joshua again one more time before he returned to Perth and she left town for good. If only she wasn't such a sucker for kids. *And their fathers,* she privately groaned. Instinct struggled with reason.

Lucy closed her eyes and endured an ache in her chest. She wanted desperately to yell out "*Yes.*" The sensible plan, of course, was not to get involved in the first place. How could she explain her caution to be selfish and maintain distance so they both escaped without broken hearts again? This was turning into a very nasty case of *déjà vu.* Oh, why did this attraction thing have to flare up now? Someone out there with a wicked sense of humor was trying to make life as difficult as possible for her at the moment.

"Lucy?" Flynn prompted over her thoughts.

"All right," she groaned reluctantly.

"You could sound a little more enthusiastic," he grumbled, grinning.

"I just hope we don't regret this."

"I won't," he said firmly. He seemed so sure it took her breath away. There was so much promise behind his words, his confidence scared her.

"Can you believe this? It makes no sense." Lucy threw her hands up in the air, laughing, then grew serious again, daring to finally say what was in her heart and on her mind. "But it's so great to be with you again."

"Mmm . . ."

"We're different people now, aren't we? After more than ten years, we still . . . connect."

"Maybe some things are meant to be," he said softly.

The subject lapsed. Lucy, for one, was blown away by the depth of her feelings for him and needed time to think.

A short while later, when he kissed her good night and watched her drive away from the house and down the long driveway in the dark, Lucy made herself a promise. She would play it by ear between now and the day she left—whether it was a day, a week, or a month—and if their fondness continued to escalate, this time around she'd make sure they dealt with the issues that still existed between them before they moved on. They hadn't done that last time. They'd been so young and had naïvely not thought beyond falling in love. They'd presumed all else would simply fall into place.

No way would she allow them to go through the same situation they'd survived before. Emotionally, it had taken her years to move on. Flynn's marriage had fallen apart. Even now, years later, she suspected her few male relationships remained casual because she was still affected by the powerful love she'd had for him and the scary fact that it still existed, to be re-awakened quickly and easily again.

Sure, she'd known they would meet and see each other again when she returned to town for George's funeral but, right from the start, Flynn had sought her out and made time for her, despite his busy working life. In his loneliness, perhaps, but there it was. Lucy didn't know what to make of it. She couldn't think too far ahead. She'd cope with Plan A for the moment and contemplate Plan B if it arose.

Her heart twinged with ironic regret for this new wonderful and just as warmly loving man she would eventually leave behind. And she *would* leave. No matter what happened, she must return to Maya. After that, her life was pretty much a blank page.

Chapter Nine

As arranged, Lucy went into Carole's salon the next day for a few hours in the morning. Although Carole was cordial toward her customers, she remained stiff with Lucy. *Who is helping her out for free!* Lucy wanted to scream. Fed up with the unfair treatment, Lucy suspected it had a cause. All ill-will usually did.

So she waited for a quiet opportunity between customers then confronted Carole.

"What exactly is your problem?" Lucy snapped. Carole squirmed, clearly caught by surprise and looking sheepish. "Spit it out. We need to clear the air."

With obvious reluctance, Carole asked, "All right then. Why didn't you come into the salon yesterday?"

Lucy frowned. "I told you, I was unavailable."

"You didn't tell me why."

"I don't believe I have to. I'm not on your payroll."

Lucy predicted what was coming. For whatever reason, Carole had a problem with her seeing Flynn again and suspected the root cause was about to emerge. After ten years, why the woman should have an issue with their renewed friendship, she had no idea. Apart from the fact that it was none of Carole's business, Lucy was more concerned with the origin of this animosity.

"I heard you were out at Flynn's all day."

Lucy folded her arms across her chest. "For once, the grapevine is accurate."

"Trying to worm your way into his affections through his son, Lucy? Really, that's low."

Lucy gasped, appalled at her friend's twisted version of the facts. "Flynn had a business meeting. He asked me to stay with Joshua. Right. Enough. This calls for action, and we can't do it here if we keep getting interrupted."

The telephone had already rung once and a customer called in to make an appointment for the following day. Irritable and determined to resolve the tension between them, which had bothered her since arriving in Mundarra, Lucy strode over to the counter, scanned the open appointment book, then scribbled a hasty note.

"What are you doing?" Carole asked, trotting after her as she stuck a notice on the salon door.

"Just letting everyone know about your family emergency." Carole gaped at her in alarm. "Don't worry, we'll concoct something by the time we get back," Lucy said forcefully. "A sick child is always a good excuse."

"Where are we going?"

"Carole, all these questions." Lucy shook her head and clicked her tongue. "Trust me."

"Where?" her friend insisted.

"The Gumnut Café."

"Why?"

"To talk. We'll grab a corner table where it's private."

"But I can't leave the salon in the middle of the day," Carole protested.

"Yes, you can." Lucy finished sticking up the notice then turned back to her friend with a thin smile. "And you will. My treat."

"I don't have the time," Carole protested, looking more afraid than upset.

"Yes, you do. We can steal a couple of hours."

"Hours!" Carole spluttered.

"We have lots to talk about." Lucy ignored Carole's protests and steered her by the elbow out the door.

"This is unnecessary and not good for my business," Carole muttered as they marched along Main Street. Lucy silently disagreed.

The Gumnut Café sat on the corner of the two main streets in town, handy for travelers and locals. A bull-nose veranda stretched across the front sheltered outdoor seating, and lace curtains hung at the full-length windows.

The bell jingled as they entered. Lucy waved to the owner, Moira Walsh, a cook of renown in the district and, leading Carole, wove among other diners to a private corner. Each table displayed fresh wildflowers in pottery vases. The replaceable white, drawing-paper tablecloths and crayons in jars for children were a unique and sensible innovation, Lucy thought, making it family-friendly.

As they seated themselves and ordered, Lucy noticed how tired and apprehensive Carole looked. Maybe she shouldn't have been quite so persuasive, but this cloud of discord hanging over their heads had to be cleared.

Since it was almost lunch time, Lucy chose Moira's homemade pumpkin soup with herbed bread and a pot of tea. Her ears pricked when Carole opted for a bowl of seafood pasta, Moira's chocolate dream cake with fudge sauce and whipped cream, and a latté. Comfort food, every mouthful. She had always been so mindful of her diet.

Lucy folded her hands on the table and started the conversation. "I appreciate that you have an opinion about my friendship with Flynn, but you need to realize it's not your concern."

"Friendship," Carole scoffed unkindly. "Is that what you call it?"

"Yes, I do." Lucy found her attitude disappointing, even a little envious and, therefore, strange.

"You can't really like him?"

Against Lucy's will, she certainly did and discovered the truth daunting, knowing she lived in another country and must eventually leave Mundarra to return overseas to her work and Maya, not knowing where that left any possible relationship with Flynn.

"Are you sure you're not rushing in?" Carole went on while Lucy processed her previous comment. "I mean, this could be a grief thing, grasping at the first affection that comes along since your father's death."

Father. Now there's a thought and another predicament. Their estranged relationship had hardly included affection.

"It looks like you're throwing yourself at him." Carole nagged. "People are talking."

Ah, *people*. Those anonymous *someones*. Lucy couldn't resist. "You mean besides yourself?" she teased. "Who?"

"Women in the salon."

"Gossips." Lucy brushed it off. "I enjoy Flynn's company. Nothing more," she hastily clarified, annoyed with herself that she felt the need to and guilty for downplaying her considerable feelings.

"Then why see him?"

A good question that Lucy struggled to answer. Fortunately, she didn't have to because their conversation paused while the waitress brought their meal, giving Lucy an opportunity to stay silent and avoid answering the question. She broke open and buttered her roll instead.

Carole twirled her fettuccine. "Are you dating Flynn or what?"

Lucy shrugged and tried to understate her involvement with him, whether out of a sense of emotional preservation or not, she wasn't sure. "We've met a few times. It's inevitable in a small town. I'm hardly going to ignore him, am I? We have a past. I'm trying to be adult about it all."

Carole grew impatient with her logic. "I can't believe you're so desperate you'd fall for his charms again. You know what Flynn Pedersen's like. It's all about money."

Enough. Lucy stung on his behalf and willingly leaped to his defense like some wild animal protecting its kin. "Actually, Flynn approached me in the first instance. And that comment is unworthy of you, Carole. Yes, he might have been work-obsessed. Once. But he's changed, and he's always been kind underneath."

Frosty and unmoved, Carole shrugged. "Well, you'd know all about that. You've been seeing him often enough. I suppose it gives you a boost to be seeing the richest man in town."

Lucy closed her eyes and gritted her teeth. The slur was not lost. Gold digger. Still single. No life. She was also beginning to see a pattern of unfair judgment behind Carole's bitter words and itched to know the cause.

Taking deep breaths before she responded, a tense silence fell between them as Lucy sipped her soup and Carole stabbed her pasta. In the pause, Lucy analyzed Carole's grumpy mood. As far as she could remember, she had never been this prickly. They'd had their share of female arguments in the past, but her recent behavior was totally out of character. There had to be a deeper problem.

"Carole, is everything all right at home?" Lucy casually dropped into the conversation.

Carole's head snapped up from eating and a moment of unguarded sadness crossed her face. Then her mask returned. "As right as a busy house with children is ever likely to be."

"Sure you're not pushing yourself too hard? Can you ease back on hours in the salon?"

"Heavens, no! It's my life."

Lucy plunged ahead before she changed her mind. "It's just that you don't seem happy. You've been snapping my head off, and I have no idea why. You were always so cheerful." She paused. "What's wrong, Cas?" she appealed gently, reverting to Carole's high school nickname.

Lucy caught the glitter of tears in her friend's eyes

before Carole hurriedly looked away across the café and out the front windows onto the quiet street beyond.

Seeing Carole upset and reluctant to speak, Lucy reached out for her hand and prompted, "Whatever it is, can I help? Or can you do something about it?"

"I don't have the courage," Carole declared in a whisper.

Lucy frowned. "Courage for what?"

"I was all right until you came back," she blurted out, glancing back at Lucy and looking guilty for the accusation. "You escaped, and I'm still stuck here."

Lucy sighed with compassion. Now they were getting somewhere.

Carole swiped at her damp cheek and pushed the plate of pasta aside, crossing her arms on the table in front of her. "I get your Christmas letters every year, and your life seems so adventurous and useful compared to mine," she grumbled. "I feel as if I haven't done anything with my life. Whereas you, you're out there saving the world. I married at nineteen, have lived in the same town all my life, then have to listen to everyone else's troubles while I do their hair."

Lucy was taken aback by her friend's revelations. "Nothing wrong with being the best hairdresser in town." When Carole flashed her a dubious glance, Lucy added, "Women talk." Which was true. Customers had praised Carole's bubbly nature and skilled hands.

"Maybe," Carole reluctantly acknowledged. "But I've never traveled and experienced the world like you have."

"Your time will come. If you want to do something badly enough, you'll find a way."

"Easy for you to say. I'll be anchored with family for

years. Oh, I adore my kids," she quickly clarified. "But I might be old and gray with no energy left before I get to have some fun."

"Fun," Lucy repeated softly. "You think my life is fun? It doesn't feel like that sometimes when I see the poverty and despair around me. At times, I don't think I can cope anymore, and I just want to pack up and leave." She smiled weakly. "Cowardly, huh? And hardly brave. I know I can't save the world alone, and I won't do UNICEF work forever, but sometimes I get so frustrated at the inequality of life. I enjoy the work and find it rewarding, but you might be surprised to know that there are moments when I wish I only had a family of my own to care about." Lucy sighed. "When I received word that George had died, I thought that time had come. I considered bringing Maya back here and settling in Mundarra again."

"Really?" Carole's distress seemed to have subsided, and she was clearly surprised.

Lucy nodded. "I thought I could try and find myself a job and put Maya in school here." Lucy wistfully recollected her plans before Daniel had dropped the disinheritance bombshell, which had deprived her of a home. She produced the photograph of Maya that was always tucked into her purse and carried with her wherever she went. She fingered the child's image now, missing her, before showing it proudly to Carole. "I think of her as my daughter."

Carole studied the photograph. "She's a sweetie. How old?"

"Six. She is a bit of a heart stopper, isn't she?" Lucy grinned with private pleasure then grew serious again.

"She's been through a lot, but she's a resilient little thing and she's recovering and settling down well after suffering the trauma of the tsunami that swept away her parents. She was only three when they died and, as far as we can find out, has no surviving close relatives. At least, no one has come forward to claim her. I wouldn't have allowed either of us to get emotionally involved until I was sure. I'd love to adopt her," she ended eagerly.

"Children can be a worry and a handful, but they make up for it with plenty of rewarding moments." Carole sighed deeply and frowned. "My problem is we never get a family holiday away together."

"You're self-employed," Lucy challenged. "Just close the shop like we did today." Seeing Carole's blank stare, she teased, "It can be done."

"It's not that simple. Roger's reliable, but he doesn't want to go anywhere."

"Then go without him." Carole's hazel eyes widened. Lucy chuckled. "I'm not kidding. He'll either jump in the car before it gets to the end of the driveway or, if he stays behind, he'll regret it, and I'll bet he goes with you the next time. Do your own thing if he has other interests."

"You make the solution sound so simple." Carole pushed out a long sigh.

When their first course plates were removed, Carole started on the chocolate dessert. Watching her friend closely, Lucy wondered if she regretted her marriage or, at least, marrying so young. "Would you want to do anything differently?" she probed. "Leave town? Study? Try another career?"

"I don't know," she moaned. "I just know all's not

right with the world in our house." She hesitated. "Despite your disagreements when you dated in high school, you and Flynn always looked right together. I guess I'm just . . . envious," she admitted in a small voice. "It's obvious you've rekindled what you both had once before. If the spark is still there, you were obviously meant to be together."

Lucy wasn't so sure about that. Yet. Embarrassed, she looked down at her hands. "I do care about him, but I'm taking it one day at a time. I have to go back to Indonesia and Maya. I promised. After that." She shrugged. "Who knows?"

Carole wrinkled her nose. "Me too. I know things have to change in our life. I just have to gather the nerve to take the first step. Roger's slack. I know that, and so does everyone else. That's who he is, and I can live with that. Although sometimes," she grinned, "I feel like putting a bomb under him. I worry that when Amy and Ben are older and leave home, we'll have nothing in common. At the moment, our daily lives operate on automatic."

"Marriage is a tricky business."

Lucy steeled herself. This was the perfect moment to confide in Carole about the developments in her mother's unfortunate marriage and Lucy's anonymous paternity. So she began slowly, and observed Carole's amazement as she unraveled all the details.

"Oh my God. Here I am blathering on about my stupid troubles, and you've got all this hanging over your head. What do you plan to do next?"

Lucy shrugged. "Wait and see if Essie Wilson contacts me."

"And if not?"

"I have no idea," she confessed despondently. "I don't know where else to look. It's not like I have any clues."

Toward the end of their successful reunion lunch, as Lucy thought of it, she said, "It's been so good talking to you about . . . everything."

"Yes, it sure helps, doesn't it?"

Lucy nodded, and they shared a knowing smile. As they left the café later, to Lucy's surprise, Carole gave her a hug before they parted. Although nothing was said, both recognized they'd reached a new understanding. The years had fallen away with the resolution of their differences, and their friendship had edged closer to what it used to be.

Lucy had arranged to meet Flynn and Joshua at the showgrounds gate. For days, townsfolk had watched a straggly assortment of caravans and trucks thunder their way into town and onto the grassy recreation reserve. Bright-colored, striped tents gradually emerged from construction chaos, and an alley of sideshow kiosks took shape. Eventually the whole showground village materialized completely, the frameworks of scary joy rides looming into the sky.

As if bestowing a seal of approval on the celebration, warm spring sunshine beamed down on everything. Now, Lucy stood and waited, filled with childish delight at spending the afternoon with who she had come to think of as her two favorite men.

Among the cavalcade of vehicles streaming and parking near the reserve—a traffic jam for Mundarra—

and an endless line of pedestrians pouring through the front gate, Lucy didn't see Flynn and Joshua arrive until a familiar boy scrambled from a four-wheel drive farther down the street and shyly grinned at her, hesitant to approach. Lucy returned his smile, waving. Then Flynn appeared at his side; Joshua took his hand and strode toward her.

Lucy's heart swelled with affection for them both, especially the ruggedly dignified man who kept his gaze firmly fixed on her until they met. Both Joshua and Flynn wore T-shirts tucked into jeans and sneakers, and Joshua wore a cap backward.

"Hey guys. Thanks for inviting me," Lucy greeted them casually.

"This is going to be fun," Joshua said, restless with excitement, missing his father's appreciative glance over Lucy's long, colorful gypsy skirt, lacy white-fitted blouse, and sensible sandals.

"Lucy," Flynn said warmly, leaning forward to publicly kiss her. Joshua darted a bright glance of interest at his father.

The revealing moment passed, and they bought tickets and filed through the gate. For a moment, adjusting to the sights and noises assaulting them from every corner—music from loud speakers, tent vendors peddling their wares, the rousing beat and sounds of marching bands—they wandered aimlessly together. An ecstatic Joshua enthused over everything. Flynn bought him a plastic windmill that twirled in the breeze as they walked.

It wasn't long before they succumbed to the tempting smells of greasy fast food and shared a bucket of fries drizzled with tomato sauce. As they stood eating, Flynn somehow managed to position himself next to Lucy as they watched a highland dancing competition in progress to the sharp skirls of bagpipes.

Despite the clamor about them, Lucy felt so attuned to the man beside her; all else ceased to exist. All noise faded as if it belonged in a dream or to another world. If he even unintentionally brushed against her, she jumped at his touch. She took a step sideways, but the awareness was still strong.

When Joshua spied the bumper cars, Lucy took the opportunity for a breather. "You two go on. I want to take a look in the Ladies' Pavilion," she indicated the long building nearby.

"Are you sure?" Flynn scowled.

"Yes." She smiled bravely. "That looks like serious men's business and no place for a woman in a skirt. I'll meet you later."

"Where?" he called after her.

"I'll find you," she assured him, disappearing indoors to the shady, more refined and beautifully displayed women's handcrafts, baking, cake decorating, and flowers.

The quiet atmosphere and low hum of mainly female voices helped restore her poise, although she failed to appreciate any of it as she found herself unable to concentrate. With each passing day, Flynn was becoming an addictive drug that she was growing to need more and more.

She felt cowardly for escaping. She who had survived living and working in remote and primitive Third World communities and villages, shrank from contact with one of the town's most upright and attractive citizens.

Lucy pulled out of her emotional distress when she recognized some ladies from Carole's salon. They briefly greeted and chatted then moved on. When she couldn't delay the reunion any longer, she emerged into the bright afternoon sunshine to see both men hanging over the fence nearby, backs turned to her, watching showjumping in the central arena. Sleek, trained horses pranced about the ring, their riders immaculately groomed in dressage outfits.

As if sensing her approach, Joshua turned. He beamed at the sight of her and tugged his father's sleeve. "Lucy's back." He thrust a huge bag of pink cotton candy toward her. "Want some?"

"Mm, yes please." She pinched off a piece of the sticky sugar fluff and felt it dissolve in her mouth. She made sure she stood on the other side of Joshua apart from Flynn.

"Are you all right?" he murmured, dipping forward past his son to glance at her.

"Yes. The pavilion is all girl stuff." She wrinkled her nose. "Didn't think you'd be interested."

Flynn ruffled his son's hair. "What do you say we hit some rides, eh, Champ?"

Joshua let out a whoop and dashed off ahead of them toward the joyrides, lost in the crowd.

"He hardly slept last night. He was so excited about today," Flynn said, seeking her hand and lacing their fingers. Lucy let herself melt a little closer to him. "He kept asking how many hours and when would he see Lucy again."

"Oh, that was sweet."

"You'll disappoint him if you avoid us," he hinted.

"Oh, I wasn't," she protested too quickly. "I thought you and Joshua should have some father and son time together."

"In this crowd?" he chuckled. "Not possible. Too much happening for an eight-year-old and his father to do any bonding."

"He idolizes you," Lucy observed.

"He leaves day after tomorrow. I'll miss him."

"Of course you will. Me too. He's a lively spark. When does he visit again?" She tried steering the conversation onto a more positive note.

"After Christmas. Summer holidays probably."

Joshua wove his way back toward them through people's legs. "Come on, Dad. It's going to stop soon. It's ten dollars and I have to ride with a grown up."

"Okay, Champ." He handed Joshua a large note. "Go buy three tickets."

"Three?" Lucy protested. "I hope you don't think—"

"I certainly do."

"That terrifying thing." Lucy looked up at the sky and the whirling buckets of screaming riders.

"We're not going without you. And you wouldn't disappoint Josh now, would you?" He flashed her a handsomely wicked grin.

"Unfair," she muttered.

It had been years since she'd braved anything so daring or even considered having anything remotely like fun. The last time she'd ridden anything as alarming as this was probably at this same show when she was eighteen at the end of high school before she had applied through the New York headquarters to work overseas with UNICEF. She and Flynn, and Carole and Roger had gone as a foursome, each couple cuddled together later in the night after dark while watching the fireworks set off from a platform out in the center of the lake.

From her daydreaming, Lucy was tugged toward the steps and up to the joyride, realizing it had ended, the last load of passengers having disembarked, windblown and laughing.

"Are you scared, Lucy?" Joshua noticed her hesitation.

"A bit," she admitted, nodding.

"Dad will look after you."

"I sure will."

He slid an arm around her waist and firmly edged her forward. They sat with Joshua between them, the safety barrier came down across the front of them, and the ride began to move. Flynn stretched out an arm behind Joshua and rested a comforting hand on Lucy's shoulder.

"You'll be fine. Why should kids have all the fun?"

"Why indeed?" Lucy's stomach filled with nerves for more than one reason.

As it happened, Lucy and Joshua screamed and laughed for the duration, but Flynn just had an amused grin plastered on his face. This man was so different to the one she'd only half-known a decade ago, and even more appealing, Lucy thought, as their ride eventually slowed and they all staggered off. He gave the impression that her presence here today was important and enjoyable for him, and she felt privileged and happy to be included in his family.

Caving to Joshua's constant pleas, the afternoon slid pleasantly by in a succession of hot dogs, warm furry cuddles in the pet nursery, dismal failure and occasional success along sideshow alley feeding balls into clowns' mouths or shooting rows of moving ducks.

By late afternoon, happily weary but moaning with aching feet, the trio strolled back to Flynn's car.

"I can find my own way back to the hotel," Lucy offered.

"After the miles we've all walked today, sounds optimistic to me. Jump in, we'll drive you."

Secretly grateful, Lucy didn't hesitate and scrambled in.

"Can Lucy come and watch the fireworks with us, Dad?" Joshua asked eagerly from the back seat as they clicked their seat belts.

Flynn eyed her speculatively. "She may have other plans."

Lucy felt a rush of embarrassment that Joshua was pressing for her continued company and Flynn might not want to offend her or disappoint his son by disagreeing.

"No," she laughed. "My appointment book is entirely free today."

Even as she accepted, Lucy knew that the more time she spent in their company, the more attached she became and wondered if it was wise. Originally, this homecoming was meant to be nothing more than attending George's funeral then leaving. She could have had no idea how lengthy her stay would become and the deep fondness that would grow from her unplanned resumption of an old friendship with her high school boyfriend. Parting promised to be a wrench. And saying good-bye to Joshua would need to be brief or she would embarrass herself with tears.

Flynn dropped her off at the hotel, arranging to call back for Lucy at seven for the fireworks. Waiting outside the Railway Hotel for their return two hours later, she wondered if Flynn recalled as vividly as she did the last time they'd watched them together. A sense of revisiting time and place resurfaced.

The two Pedersen men arrived, Flynn held the door open, then they were on their way again. At the lake, Joshua hauled a huge tartan rug across to the grass and spread it out for them.

Although she was probably being over-sensitive, Lucy was aware how it must look to people, especially those immediately nearby. The three of them forming a cozy family unit. Flynn seemed blissfully ignorant of any extended looks they received. He knew most of the locals, greeting and chatting to them politely, introducing Lucy to those who did not know or remember her. She silently endured the unspoken speculation, grateful for the privacy of darkness.

When the first fireworks popped, other spectators in front stood for a better look, forcing Lucy and Flynn to stand too, so they didn't miss any of it. Joshua had wriggled away from them, closer to the lake's edge for a clear view with a group of other children.

As the display burst into stars and showers of color overhead, Flynn stepped behind Lucy and slid his arms around her waist, nestling his face into her hair. It seemed the most natural gesture in the world and a heartening end to the day, as much as she still feared the consequences of opening her heart. They'd had no time alone together, and Lucy discovered she missed the warmth and reassurance of being close to him. It was hardly private there amid a crowd, but luckily all eyes were focused on the festivities lighting up the night sky, not on Flynn Pedersen giving his old girlfriend a cuddle, so she tried to relax and enjoy it.

When Flynn drove her back to the hotel, he said to his sleepy son, "Stay here, Champ. I'll only be five minutes," and walked Lucy to her room.

At the door, she said, "Thanks for a fabulous day."

"It has been, hasn't it?" He caught her hand and squeezed it. "No news yet?"

Lucy shook her head.

"What if you never find out?"

"I'll be devastated." She shrugged. "Unfinished business."

"It could happen that way," he warned her gently.

"I know," she sighed.

"If it does, don't keep looking back."

Lucy frowned. "I'll have to. Keep searching and trying."

"I understand how you must feel. Just be careful you don't miss your whole life in the process. If there's one thing I've learned since my divorce it's that you have to move on."

"What if I can't?" she whispered dismally. "What if I never find out."

"One day at a time."

Sage advice. "Of course."

"So," he paused, "I guess you're staying on a while longer."

She nodded.

In the dimly lit hallway, Flynn placed a finger under her chin, drew her into his arms, and kissed her with serious longing. "Josh is spending tomorrow with his grandparents and cousins, but he'll want to say good-bye to you the day after that."

"I hate long good-byes," she confessed.

"Don't we all," he murmured, kissing her again.

"Maybe just a phone call?" she suggested. Although it was pleasurable to linger, she added, "You'd better go. Joshua will be wondering where you are."

"What are the odds he's already asleep?"

"High." They shared a grin.

"You're good with kids."

Lucy shrugged. "I certainly love being around them. I've had plenty of experience."

"Because of your unhappy childhood?"

"Undoubtedly. But after what I've witnessed overseas, I realize it could have been so much worse. At least I had a roof over my head and plenty of food."

"I have another meeting tomorrow, but I'll be in touch. Good night."

He strode down the hallway. She leaned against the door frame, half hoping he'd turn and give her one last smile or wave, but he didn't and disappeared from view. She sighed and turned the key in the lock.

Chapter Ten

"Lucy?"

She had experienced a few bittersweet good-byes in her life. Leaving Maya had certainly been one of them, but when she heard Joshua's tentative, small voice on the other end of the telephone the next day, her heart twisted with empathy.

Rallying, she forced a brightness into her voice she certainly didn't feel. "Hey, Champ. Great to hear from you again."

"Dad said I only have five minutes. We're driving down to Melbourne soon." He sounded despondent.

"You'll have heaps to tell your mum."

There was a pause. "She won't care."

In the face of such disheartenment, Lucy found it hard to stay positive. "I'm sure she does. Not everyone can show it. When are you coming back to visit your dad?"

"Holidays, I guess."

"That's not so far away. Every day will bring you closer to returning."

"Dad bought me a Gecko."

Lucy drew a blank. "A pet?"

Her unintentional blunder raised a giggle from Joshua, and the conversation took a lighter turn.

"No, silly. It's a mobile phone just for kids. It's got emergency numbers and Dad's numbers so I can call him whenever I want." Normal excitement reflected in his voice again.

"Sounds a great way to keep in touch."

Despite the huge physical distance between father and son, Flynn was certainly making every effort to ensure their communication was easy. Lucy's respect for him increased now that he seemed more proactive in being a part of Joshua's life. When she'd first arrived, Flynn had sounded bitter and helpless that his son lived so far away.

"I asked Dad to put in your number, but he didn't know it. He said they might not have phones where you live in Indonesia."

She smiled. "They do, but not very many. But I gave you my e-mail address, remember?"

"Yep."

"I expect you to write and tell me everything you're doing back home. I'll be waiting for an e-mail in my in-box by the time I return to Indonesia, okay? Think you can manage that?"

"Sure."

There were voices and background noises; Lady barked with excitement.

"Dad says we have to go." Lucy heard the panic in his voice then, changing tone, heard him whisper down the line, "My dad likes you."

"Does he?" She was speechless. "That's nice."

"He said you're a very special woman." Lucy felt herself blush over the innocently revealed words. "I want to stay with my dad here, but he said I have to go back to my mum."

"You'll be back soon. Count down the days and sleeps," Lucy said encouragingly, relieved to be off the heartrending subject of Flynn and his personal feelings.

"You won't be here next time, will you?"

"No, that's right," she said gently. "You remember Maya. She's my family like your dad and mum are your family. I need to get back to her too. You understand that, don't you?"

"I guess."

His barely audible voice tugged at her heartstrings. "Families come in all shapes and sizes. It's important we keep in touch with our family wherever they are."

"I guess." He didn't sound particularly convinced by her words of wisdom. "I gotta go." A sense of urgency entered his voice. "Dad's started the car."

"Okay, Champ. Have a good trip. I loved spending time with you. Bye for now."

"Bye, Lucy," he said hurriedly, then the phone went dead with a sudden click. Lucy held on to the receiver a moment longer, nostalgic, before she hung up too.

When another challenging telephone call came two days later from Essie Wilson, it was unexpected and far sooner than Lucy had either anticipated or dared hope. The older woman didn't explain why she was inviting Lucy to Roseleigh for afternoon tea. There was no need. The reason was implicit. Whatever had transpired in Lucy's mother's youth would finally be revealed.

As Lucy walked up the garden pathway of the Wilson family home for the second time in weeks, battling the changeable spring wind, her stomach was sick with apprehension. Whatever she learned today, at least she would know.

Essie sat in one of two old-fashioned, white cane chairs beside a table in the shade of the broad veranda. Distracted by the enticing confusion of the large wilderness garden, Lucy didn't notice her until a movement caught her eye.

Essie rose and greeted her with an unsteady smile. "Lucy, I'm pleased you've come."

"Thank you for inviting me."

When they had dealt with the pleasantries and Lucy was comfortably seated in the other chair, she practiced deep breathing and waited patiently while Essie went through the ritual of pouring tea.

On the one hand, Lucy wanted to shake the information from her. Get it out. Know. On the other, she felt anxious knots tie up her stomach and wanted to approach it gradually. Ease toward it and give herself time to think and adjust.

This was obviously Essie's logical strategy and was clearly in tune with her fastidious personality. Each had waited decades for the truth, both to receive and divulge it. What was another five minutes?

"What I'm about to tell you," Essie said as she handed Lucy a filled teacup, "I've kept in confidence as a promise to your mother for over thirty-five years."

Lucy grew sick and tense and excited.

"Even now, I'm not sure I should break that confidence." Essie twisted a lace handkerchief in her hands. "But it seems the time has come. There are things you should know. Probably should have known five years ago after your mother died. But all the involved parties have now passed on and, in light of George's recent will, secrecy hardly seems relevant."

Because Essie seemed even more nervous than Lucy, she didn't interrupt.

"I should feel free to speak, but somehow I still feel like I'm betraying your mother's memory and good name. If George hadn't disinherited you, I might have wrongfully taken this information to my grave. I can see now that would have been a mistake." Essie gave her a long, steady glance and her hand shook as she sipped her tea. "I'll tell you your father's name, then I'll explain."

Lucy nodded, filled with dread and anticipation.

Essie set down her cup with a clatter. "Lucy, dear, you and I, although from different generations, are half-sisters. My father Theodore Wilson was also your father."

Lucy's heart pounded while her head wrapped around the stunning information. Her mother's boss. "What?" she rasped out in a whisper.

Unhurried, as if allowing Lucy to digest the information, Essie offered her a gingersnap biscuit. Lucy accepted out of politeness but, sick to her stomach, knew she couldn't eat a thing.

"You know Marion worked for my father at Wilson's Emporium for many years," Essie said, immediately continuing. "My grandfather, Alfred Wilson, started it in the early days of the twentieth century selling everything from blacking to perfumed water, bolts of material to kerosene lamps. He amassed considerable wealth and built Roseleigh. My—our—father, Theo, was his only son and groomed to succeed." Essie's gaze drifted out across the garden. "He was a debonair man."

"I only vaguely remember him." Lucy's mind tumbled with confusion, still grasping the reality of what Essie had just revealed. Theo Wilson, renowned Mundarra businessman, was her father. And this lovely lady she'd known all her life was a half-sister. *Family.*

The older woman reached out a hand to cover Lucy's and smiled weakly. "Don't worry. I'll show you photographs, and we'll talk. I have so much more to tell you." Her face turned reflective in memory. "Father always wore his trademark pinstriped suits and strutted importantly about the store. His public image was of a respected businessman beyond reproach. A civic minded gentleman with an elegant, dutiful wife and three daughters. No sons to carry on the family name. Always my father's deepest regret. If you'd been a boy," Essie darted a rueful glance at Lucy, "he might have claimed you."

Essie sighed. "I don't know if that's how or why he came to despise my mother. I suspect he married her because Beatrice Rowland was a respectable doctor's daughter and even further enhanced his standing in town. For whatever reason, in later years, my father became a philanderer. Mother may have known or suspected but ignored his adultery. Father was discreet. He was a suave rascal," she said, shaking her head almost in admiration. "Yet he discouraged any of our suitors.

He claimed none of them were good enough for his daughters. Any young man who showed the slightest interest was swiftly dispatched to greener female pastures.

"Father was dominant, accustomed to control. With a household of women in those days it wasn't hard. We weren't raised to defy him, and certainly none of us was rebellious enough to try. Although my oldest sister, Caroline, briefly pursued a secret relationship. She was so happy for a while," Essie sighed. "But afraid of being discovered. Which of course she was. Father crushed the alliance. Caroline always had delicate health and, within five years, she'd pined away. I always believed she died of a broken heart," she said fiercely, her mouth a thin line.

The memories tumbled easily from Essie's mouth, so Lucy just listened. It was, after all, her stepfamily and she was interested to learn more, but it also seemed to be therapeutic for the other woman to share it all.

"Soon after Caroline died, our mother died suddenly too. I worked sometimes in the store when needed, but mostly I kept house for our father. My other sister, Mary, loved the garden. Since she's been gone these past ten years, the grounds have suffered. As you can see." Essie spread an arm wide. "I don't have the interest or energy to restore them. It was a showplace garden while Mary and our gardener worked on it. I suspect my sister had a fondness for him and that was a large part of her pleasure in it. Grandmother Wilson, Mary, and my mother all loved the garden, especially roses. That's how the house was named."

Lucy drew in a steady breath, bewildered by all this new family information.

"After mother's death, father turned his charm upon Marion. As my friend she was here at Roseleigh often, of course. As the most senior associate and a long-serving employee, she sometimes accompanied him to business functions. Father obviously had his sights set on her as his next conquest, and the attraction on her part quickly developed. He gradually flattered and won her. He was a master of seduction and Marion, like every woman, was powerless to resist him. Even in his fifties, father was extremely handsome and looked years younger.

"I expect Marion believed she loved father but, in reality, it was only a deep infatuation because of his attentions. Be assured Lucy, dear, he may have expertly seduced her but she was a willing participant. When she became pregnant she went to him."

Essie paused but Lucy was anxious for her to continue, finding the whole background story fascinating. "What did he say?"

"To save his reputation he contrived a solution. At that time, of course, George McCarthy was interested in Marion, so my father approached him with a generous financial offer to marry her and make her respectable." Essie smiled sadly. "Marion always thought he must have cared deeply for her to go to such lengths to protect her, but he was just saving his own skin. He paid for an expensive engagement ring."

Lucy's heart lurched. The one a certain Mrs. McCarthy now owned, she thought bitterly, that clearly belonged to Theo and Marion's only descendant. Her.

"He also paid for their wedding and bought the house in Deacon Street for George and Marion to live in. All on the understanding that his name would never be revealed and that George would be publicly acknowledged as your father."

"Their marriage was a business deal!" While he may have been self-serving, at least Theo Wilson hadn't neglected those for whom he held responsibility.

"I'm sorry, my dear. It all sounds so heartless, but I can assure you it's all exactly as Marion told me and she accepted the situation. Even in the early Seventies when feminism and women's voices were growing stronger, the old stigmas still existed. Marion wanted respectability and security. She tolerated George as a husband and an escape from her predicament, but she certainly never loved him."

"I gathered that much over the years. Ours was a dysfunctional, unloving family," Lucy said poignantly.

"You look so much like your mother, suspicion was never cast on George's paternity. His heritage was always a bit of a mystery. Marion said he never disclosed anything about his family background."

"No, never." Lucy shook her head, realizing how little they had known about him. And she found she no longer cared.

"Marion said that his birth certificate said he was born in Fitzroy. Perhaps he left the working class suburb to get ahead in life."

"I don't care where he came from or want to know anything about him. I doubt it's even of any interest to Michael. It's definitely no longer of any concern to me."

"You would remember your grandmother Greenwood though, wouldn't you? Marion's mother."

"Yes. She visited a few times when I was small. Ironically, I've recently changed my name to Greenwood. Now that I've discovered who I really am." Lucy pulled a wry grin.

"Whether you ever publicly acknowledge your Wilson ancestry is up to you, my dear. I would be quite proud and comfortable if you made that decision."

"I may. I need more time to think about it and digest all this."

"Of course. You might want to pursue your Greenwood heritage too. I can put you in touch with distant relations if you like."

"Oh, yes, please." Lucy grasped at the opportunity. "I've been feeling so lost as far as family is concerned since all of this blew up. I'd welcome any connection."

Essie heaved a wistful sigh. "The woman you knew as your mother wasn't the *real* Marion Greenwood. Not the happy, carefree soul that was my dearest friend. I wish you'd known her when she was really young, before everything happened and she married." Essie studied Lucy for a moment. "You have some of our father's ways about you, but you mostly resemble your mother. Although Marion was quite lovely, she always considered you far more beautiful. She was so proud of you."

Lucy filled with a deep sadness. "She never told me. Mother was always a closed book."

"She changed after her marriage. She probably felt reluctant to spoil you in front of George, under the circumstances. You were her daughter, a love child, and deeply cherished because of it, even if she never felt able to tell you. She was terrified of George. He threatened to cast you both out if she didn't keep their secret."

"And all along, the sneaky old devil was unfaithful himself and deliberately plotted to disown us," Lucy muttered.

Essie nodded. "He was a cunning man. When you didn't come to me after your mother died, I knew she'd never told you about your father. My dilemma ever since has been whether I should be the one to tell you the truth. Marion swore me to secrecy."

"Oh, Essie. I'm so glad you did." Lucy laughed through the tears that filled her eyes at the absurdity of the situation. "Just when I thought I was homeless and adrift, I have a home and family after all. I'll return to visit. I promise." Just how she would manage it, she had no idea, but she would certainly try. Lucy eagerly leaned forward in her chair. "I want you to tell me more about my mother, your family and . . . my father." She found the word awkward to say.

"Of course, dear." Rising from her seat, Essie glanced at the clouds thickening overhead. "The weather's turning. Come into the house."

Lucy's jaw dropped as she and Essie moved from the veranda indoors, gradually wandering the large Roseleigh rooms. Their chatty murmurs and footsteps echoed through the grand but cavernous house. Gracious wrought iron bedsteads. Marble fireplaces. Ornate trimmings. It had obviously been built in an era of big families and was crying out to be filled again.

Her half-sister, twice her age and who she viewed in a whole new light, pointed out special features, the significance and history behind certain pieces of solid dark furniture, heavily framed black-and-white photographic portraits, including one of her father, Theo, in his youth and various exquisite antiques and artifacts about the house.

"You can come here any time to chat and roam," Essie offered. "This is your family home too now." She paused in the wide-tiled hallway and hesitantly grasped one of Lucy's hands. "I've watched you from afar since you were born, knowing you were part of my family and wishing you could be in my life. Hoping you might one day want to be, if and when you ever learned about your real father."

"Absolutely." Because Essie looked lost, Lucy impulsively hugged her, knowing the emotional risk it must have cost her to reveal the truth.

As soon as Essie led her toward the back of the house through the huge renovated cream and timber kitchen, Lucy fell even more deeply in love with the house.

Hearing her gasp and seeing the pleasure in her face, Essie smiled warmly. "Special, isn't it? I spend most of my time out here."

The glass sitting room cum conservatory beyond was *her* kind of room. With its black-and-white tiled floor, stuffed sofas, and masses of potted plants, it overlooked the untended rear garden and ancient trees sweeping their branches to the unmown lawn beneath.

As they looked out through the French doors, the garden was touched now by a shower of rain, dripping with moisture. Damp and lovely.

"Oh," Essie beamed. "It's so much more fun finally being able to share all this."

Sheltering under an umbrella borrowed from Essie against the light misty rain that had begun to fall, Lucy closed the gate on Roseleigh and hurriedly strode back to the hotel, her mind still dazed from everything her half-sister had told her. She shivered in the wind and rain that had swept in, unused to such chilly weather.

Her father was Theodore Wilson! Her chest burst with relief, not to mention astonishment that her prim mother had so passionately loved a man that Lucy had been the result. Even if her father had been a womanizing rascal, at least he had supported Marion financially and helped set her up in a new life. Unfortunately, it was destined to be a disastrous alliance.

Because she itched to confide this important revelation, Lucy's first instinct was to contact Flynn. She almost turned her footsteps in the direction of Mundarra Motors but hesitated. As much as she had grown to care about the man again, she still held deep reservations for any future between them. Besides, dripping wet and in emotional turmoil was probably not the best time or a good look for an earnest discussion. Which she suspected her next meeting with Flynn would become.

Now that she had learned the truth about her heritage, there was no reason to stay in Mundarra. She could return home to Indonesia. She contemplated the word *home*, knowing that at the moment neither Asia nor Australia felt like it. She had loved ones in both places now, and her loyalties were torn between two continents.

Before she could decide where to settle, she would need some sign that propelled her in one direction or the other. More and more, since being exposed to other religions and cultures, Lucy believed in karma, though it didn't always sit well with her natural spontaneous tendencies, catapulting her off in unplanned directions.

So the thought of waiting for an indication of where her future lay was frustrating.

Firstly, it was unquestionable that she must return to Indonesia for Maya and set adoption wheels in motion. Once those proceedings were underway, of all her options and plans, Lucy's deepest wish was to return to Australia permanently and raise Maya with all the love and security she had been denied by a disastrous, once-in-a-century freak of nature.

Back at the hotel and after a warm shower, Lucy dressed, toweled her hair dry and restlessly paced her claustrophobic room. Giving in to her strong compulsion, she grabbed the telephone, pressed a button for an outside line and dialed Flynn's work number. Put on hold, she almost changed her mind and hung up.

"Pedersen," he announced suddenly.

"It's Lucy."

His voice warmed. "Good morning."

"Um . . . Essie phoned."

After the briefest silence, he asked, "Where are you?"

"In my hotel room."

"Stay put. I'll be right there."

Anxious for more than one reason, Lucy waited outside under the hotel veranda listening to the steady rain on its iron roof. Within minutes, she saw the familiar four-wheel drive appear and glide to a stop. Flynn reached across the front seat and opened the passenger door.

"Thanks for coming," she said breathlessly as she slid in out of the rain and fastened her seat belt, brushing moisture from her clothes.

He sent her a gentle gaze. "You can ask anything of me any time."

Oh Lord, Lucy melted. Parting promised to be a nightmare. They sped off. Deeply preoccupied in her own whirling thoughts and sadness about leaving, she didn't take any notice of where they were headed until she realized they were out in the country and pulled into a roadside picnic stop. Flynn nosed the vehicle up to a wire farm fence so they looked out through rivulets of raindrops running down the windscreen. Beyond lay a sheep paddock with isolated stands of sheltering eucalypts and low distant hills. Flynn turned off the motor, and they were plunged into silence, the only sound the gentle patter of raindrops on the car roof.

Lucy drew in a deep, slow breath as Flynn turned toward her. "My real father was Theodore Wilson, mother's boss."

He gave a low, soft whistle and reached across the automatic gear shift, seeking her hand and clasping it between his own. His reassuring touch helped her continue and explain the background as Essie had related it to her only hours before, including the clinical manner of George and Marion's union.

"An arranged marriage." Flynn shook his head in disbelief. "You're a Wilson. Old Theo and your mother. Incredible." He eyed Lucy cautiously. "How do you feel about all this?"

Lucy shrugged, still bewildered by it all. "Shocked, at first. Then kind of strange. Weird to think of Essie as my half-sister. Then eventually I felt pleased that mother at least experienced one romance in her life even if it was brief and meant nothing to my father. I'm trying to believe that he felt something for her in their relationship. In my mind, it helps compensate for the lack of love in her marriage to George."

"So, you're really Lucy Wilson," Flynn remarked.

She sighed. "Yes, I guess I am. And if Essie's representative of the family, then I'm proud to be part of it. After Daniel confronted me with the disinheritance and paternity bombshells, I felt lost. Now I feel part of a family again." Two families, actually, since Flynn had so readily welcomed her into his life. How lucky could a girl get?

Flynn clenched his jaw and turned away, growing reflective, and withdrew his hand from hers. Lucy assumed her talk of family must have evoked thoughts of Joshua.

"Friends may come and go, and life changes, but family is all important, isn't it?"

He nodded. "Certainly is."

"Have you heard from Joshua since he got back to Perth?"

He shook his head. "Only been a few days, and his mother will discourage it."

Lucy smiled sadly for him. "He told me about his Gecko, so that will make it easier to be in touch when he can."

Flynn scowled and drummed his fingers on the steering wheel. "I hope so. That's why I bought it. He didn't want to leave this time. That's a positive. The boy's had enough upset in his life. I'm trying to create stability for him, at least while he's with me. He doesn't seem to get much of it living with his mother."

"You don't need to be in one place for Joshua to feel secure. You just need to be there for him. You can give a child love anywhere. You're a good person and a great role model. That's all Joshua needs to see."

"I really regret not having a successful marriage," Flynn admitted. "First time around," he added with meaning. Lucy guessed he was referring to their renewed attraction for each other and the possibility of where it could lead.

She thrilled to the private knowledge. "Knowing you, I'm sure you tried. Not all families are destined to be happy."

"I failed simply because I couldn't love Sandy." He turned to face her, his voice soft, his expression anguished. "Do you have any idea why, Lucy?"

A stirring of suspicion entered her mind but she dared not voice it, so she shook her head instead and stayed silent.

"Sandy wasn't you. I still loved you when I married her and that was wrong and selfish of me."

"Oh," Lucy whispered, dejected to notice he had used the past tense.

After seeing him again, despite the intervening years, it was clear Flynn would never be edged from that special place in her heart. Sometimes somebody touches your life in some way, even for the briefest time, and you never forget them. It was exactly like that with him. She'd only realized after she left Mundarra that her high school crush had really been much more. Now, by his own admission, he had once really and truly loved her; even hinted at more, and she felt almost burdened by the weight of his suggestion.

Hopeful but terrified, Lucy wondered where on earth they could go from here.

"We never seem to quite connect, do we, Lucy?"

She nodded, smiling, but was desperately confused and miserable inside. "Last time you were young and filled with a restless independence. This time, you're just passing through. You enjoy your UNICEF work, don't you?"

"Yes." Lucy couldn't lie and hastily added, "But I guess I won't always be doing it."

"You won't? You'd find it hard to settle down," he speculated.

"Perhaps. Perhaps not." Lucy had no idea how long or complicated Maya's adoption process might be. In case there was some problem, she decided not to mention her definite plans to return to Australia. It was nice knowing Flynn was settled in Mundarra and would still be here when she returned for good. "But life goes in phases. One stage closes, another opens. Most people are adaptable to that." Too subtle? Flynn Pedersen was a savvy bloke. Surely he caught her meaning.

"So, my time here is nearly over." Lucy tried to sound bright and philosophical.

"When do you leave?"

"As soon as I book my travel arrangements, I guess."

"You'll want to get back to Maya?"

Lucy nodded, an excited maternal pull already growing to see her beautiful girl again. Even though they weren't yet officially a family, she longed for it to be soon.

"I'd like to stay in touch," was all he said.

In touch? Well, that was something. "Sure. I'll give you my address and phone number." She forced a smile. "That would be nice."

Nice? She could slap herself for sounding so pathetic. She'd probably just passed up a great opportunity to declare her love. But she didn't want to sound too eager or pushy. On the other hand, if he asked, she'd jump into his lap right now. *Please give me hope, Flynn,* she silently pleaded. *A reason to come back. Not to Mundarra or Essie. To you and Joshua. The smallest hint. Something to cling to.* She held her breath and waited for him to say something, but no pleas or promises came.

When his mobile phone sang out a catchy tune, Lucy wanted to tear if from his hands and toss it out of the car window.

He grimaced. "Sorry. Excuse me."

He stepped from the vehicle and took the call. She hadn't noticed, but the rain had stopped and she tried not to appear too miserable as she contemplated the wet landscape. Interrupted by his untimely phone call, she knew any moment of opportunity had been well and truly lost. He may still care for her but apparently not enough for him to ask her to stay. The crushing knowledge nearly drove her to tears.

When Flynn slid in behind the wheel again, his previously intimate mood had vanished, replaced by his familiar businesslike efficiency.

"Dramas in the office. I'm needed," he apologized with a rueful smile.

Story of her life. Flynn's work always took priority. Why should now be any different? She frowned. Her overseas social work had been important too. Once. In the last few years since fostering Maya, her priorities had gradually and subtly changed. Her love of full-time welfare work was being replaced by a deeper need to settle in one place, have her own little nest.

With even the slightest indication from Flynn, she would give up her UNICEF work in a heartbeat for him. Their relationship had stalled once before through lack of understanding and communication. She should just put herself out there and not let her feminine pride control her expectations of a knight riding up on his white charger to claim her and whisk her away.

Nothing further was said on their return drive into town, rain still pelting down, the wipers working madly all the way.

When he stopped in front of the hotel, he turned off the engine. "I'll miss you. I've liked having you back in my life."

"Me too." Lucy's hopes rose. Maybe there was a chance after all. "I loved meeting Joshua and getting to know him."

"Thanks for spending time with him." He eyed her steadily, and the pauses in their conversation grew longer.

"My pleasure."

He let out a soft moan and suddenly leaned across, one hand on the nape of her neck tangling his fingers in her mass of thick hair, to give her a stunning kiss of passionate desperation, leaving her breathless and aching with unvoiced love. So many times she'd almost blurted it out, but the wariness of exposing herself to hurt again held her back. Not to mention her uncertain immediate future. Talk about a catch-22.

Neither spoke, but their long, shared gaze spoke volumes. A few moments later, she could only smile weakly and miserably watch him drive away, her heart twisting with loss.

Chapter Eleven

The next day in her hotel room, Lucy was an emotional mess. Leaving was going to hurt. Her own fault, of course. She had been foolish to give her heart away. Again. To the same man. She wanted to childishly stamp her feet in frustration, but she knew better than to waste the energy.

Like a robot, she operated on automatic, sorting and packing her things. From the library Internet terminal she had e-mailed the UNICEF travel unit, and her flight from Melbourne was arranged and confirmed, setting an irrevocable seal on her return to Indonesia late tomorrow.

Tonight she had a family dinner scheduled with Carole but, meanwhile, to keep occupied and because she felt a deep need, she headed east from town toward the cemetery where they had buried George only weeks before.

Standing before her mother's grave, a gusty current of air streamed the long hair back from Lucy's face and

167

shoulders. She placed fresh roses from Essie's garden on the newly erected headstone.

Hugging herself against the brisk wind whipping across the quiet, isolated site, she murmured, "I'm sorry you couldn't tell me about my father. I wish you'd been a stronger person. I wish you'd never met George. And, above all, I wish you'd had a happier life." She kissed her fingers and blew a kiss. "Sweet dreams, Mum."

Lucy gazed out across the paddocks of dry yellow stubble to the random stands of gums, screeching parrots flitting among eucalypt branches. She breathed in deeply their minty scent and inhaled the essence of Mundarra deep into her soul. Who knew when she might be back. She had friends and, now, family here; emotional attachments but no compelling reason to specifically return here anytime soon.

Apprehensive to face Flynn again for fear of making a blathering fool of herself and confessing her love, and guessing his kiss last night that had rocked her soul was, actually, good-bye, she left the borrowed car at the hotel and the keys with the receptionist.

That evening, Lucy walked the short distance around to Carole's home for dinner, grateful for the company and preoccupation on her last night in town. They feasted on a sumptuous roast dinner followed by lattice apple pie and cream. She played cards with Amy and Ben while Carole and Roger stacked the dishwasher and cleaned up in the kitchen. Then, with the children in bed early before another school day, the three adults sipped wine and ate chocolate while reminiscing.

Throughout the evening, Lucy was heartened to witness more of the old bubbly Carole emerging; whereas, the whole time, Lucy herself was all too aware of the one person missing with whom she longed to share the occasion. As a result, she drank more than her share of the rosé to numb her pain. Because she'd obviously over-indulged to become sleepily happy, Carole drove Lucy back to the hotel, and they embraced in a long warm hug before parting.

"See you in the morning." Carole waved, and Lucy watched the red tail lights of her car disappear down the street. She'd never felt lonelier in her life.

He wasn't here. Flynn hadn't come. Lucy slunk lower into her bus seat, unable to resist furtive glances out of the windows, just in case. The least Flynn could have done was surprise her and show up. You didn't kiss a woman the way he had two nights ago without feeling something way more than casual. It had been so deep and intense, leaving her in no doubt that she was loved. But he was a no-show.

She felt abandoned and her departure like unfinished business. Spending time with Flynn and Joshua had made Lucy realize what was missing in her life. A family of her own.

But she couldn't abandon Maya. She'd promised to return. She loved the child and had felt a special bond from the moment she had set eyes on the waif, lost and crying, one of tens of thousands similarly destitute after the tsunami floodwaters had receded, revealing horrendous devastation. Lucy's heart had instinctively opened, and Maya's tiny arms had wrapped tightly around her neck. The pair had been inseparable ever since.

Lucy smiled bravely on the outside through the bus

window at Carole and Essie huddled in a brave bunch on the pavement but was miserable with disappointment inside.

The bus engine rumbled into life and idled for a few minutes before the heavy vehicle slowly pulled away. She was leaving. She flashed a last bright wave and smile at her tiny knot of friends, growing smaller as the bus moved farther down the street that joined the highway from town.

Lucy's last night in Mundarra had been restless. Once she boarded her flight in Melbourne and headed north across Australia and the Timor Sea, perhaps her misery would ease.

When her mobile phone beeped she was surprised to read a text message from Flynn. *Thinking of you*. Lucy frowned over the obscure message. Without committing herself either, she merely replied: *Ditto*.

In the hours it took to reach the airport, Lucy's mind blanked, her emotions on automatic. Occasionally, she dozed. She moved mechanically through the crowds all boarding planes, restlessly moving around the world. It should have cheered her that global travel was so common these days and she could always return. It was not knowing where she belonged anymore that was her biggest dilemma.

As the small plane Flynn had hired at Medan made its final approach before landing on the tiny remote airfield in northern Sumatra, he and Joshua shared a conspiratorial smile and a thumbs up sign.

For the entire flight, the scenery had been a breathtaking fusion of pristine seawater and dense vegetation, at least from above, providing an image of lush tropical tranquillity below.

The aircraft made a bumpy landing along the grassy strip and rolled to a stop. Joshua and Flynn stepped out into the steamy warmth, hauling their bags with them. Their taxi, a beaten-up vehicle that had seen far better days, took them through a small town past bicycles, pedestrians, tricycles with baskets stacked with all manner of goods and foods, and out along narrow sealed roads riddled with potholes and hugged either side by lush greenery.

When they reached the village, Flynn paid the smiling driver and they clambered out. They stood disoriented by the roadside looking about them, the focus of wary gazes from locals. With a combination of sign language, inadequate Indonesian, and good luck they were directed farther along the main street of houses, shops, and a mosque toward a small neat wooden house with a front porch, its door and windows flung open, as most seemed to be.

A dog barked nearby, and a girl played out front with a handful of rocks and stones, laying them out in patterns on the ground.

"That's Maya," Joshua whispered, looking up at his father, eyes glinting with joy.

The beautiful brown-eyed, olive-skinned girl had silky straight black hair trailing over her shoulders. Except for her dark complexion, Flynn marveled at the fact that she could have been Lucy's own natural daughter, they looked so much alike.

"Looks like we've come to the right place, eh, Champ? Let's go in."

Seeing the broad smile of greeting on Maya's face when she'd returned to her village in Indonesia two months ago had helped ease Lucy's pain of separation from others she also loved.

She threw herself back into her work and started official adoption proceedings for Maya, all of which helped distract her from thoughts of Flynn, but he was never far from her mind. So when she heard a voice that sounded like his, she briefly stopped working and lifted her head to listen but gave herself a mental shake. Impossible. Imagination was a teasing visitor, so she ignored the fantasy and continued hoeing in the vegetable plot behind her humble rented house.

Until Maya breathlessly dashed toward her along the garden path. "*Ibu. Ibu. Lebih aneh*," she said excitedly, her almond eyes bright, long black hair flying out behind her as she ran.

In her delight, Maya had called her *mother* as usual but in her native tongue.

"Strangers?" Lucy repeated, frowning. Could be a former colleague but, in their familiarity, they would have called out to her. And Maya had definitely said strangers, so it was no one she knew.

Her small dark head nodded. "Man and boy. Not Maya's people. Mamma's people."

At the unbelievable possibility, the hoe slid from Lucy's hands and dropped onto the ground. She strode back to the house with Maya skipping excitedly around her, a vague soaring hope lodged in her heart and mind.

It couldn't be! She forced down the nerves of anticipation, washed her hands in the water dish by the back door, and walked slowly through to the front of the house, Maya now shyly one step behind like a shadow.

She recognized them before she emerged from the dim interior and out into the baking sunshine. Both man and boy wore T-shirts, khaki camouflage shorts, and sensible walking sandals.

Disbelief at the sight of them eclipsed questions and the reasons for their unexpected appearance on her doorstep. Lucy and Maya halted on the front porch. Everyone stared at each other, and smiles wreathed every face.

Suddenly, Joshua launched himself at her. "Surprise, Lucy." He beamed.

She bent to scoop him up in a fierce hug, laughing. Over his head her magnetic gaze was drawn to his father and stayed. Joshua loosened his grip and, as one, he and Lucy focused on Flynn who dropped his bag and strolled slowly forward.

"Tell me you're not lost," Lucy breathed.

He shook his head. "Not anymore."

"Not on your way to somewhere else?"

He shook his head again, and she raised a steadying hand to cover her gaping mouth, blinking back tears of delirious joy. She had missed him so much. "This is the best surprise I've ever had in my life."

As though they had all the time in the world, their arms slid around each other and they just stood still, locked together in the warmth of a mutual, welcoming embrace. She had a good idea what this visit meant. Obviously, Flynn had come for her! But she did not know how long they could stay, so she planned to enjoy every second and not dwell on negatives.

Feeling a pair of warm arms clinging to her loose cotton trousers, Lucy pulled away from Flynn and looked down, smiling.

"Maya." She stooped and wrapped a reassuring arm around the girl's shoulder. "This is Flynn and Joshua. My friends from Australia."

Maya looked overawed and smiled. Upon her return to Indonesia, Lucy had related where she'd been and explained as simply as possible only what she thought the child could understand and absorb.

The girl clapped her hands and repeated, "Yosh."

Amid their laughter, Lucy grew serious and turned to Flynn, asking soberly, "How long can you stay?"

"Two weeks." His gaze lingered over her. "I have Joshua for part of the summer holidays."

It was amazing that they had come all this way so see her. She could hardly wait until she and Flynn had an opportunity to talk alone later.

"Come inside," she beckoned.

"Do you have room for us?" Flynn looked uncertainly toward the small house.

"It's basic, but we have everything we need." She smiled in reassurance. "If you find you're not comfortable," she added, "I won't be offended if you prefer to stay in a local hotel. But the accommodation might not be a lot better." She chuckled.

Flynn gently laid a hand on her arm. "We came to see *you*," he emphasized, and she filled with relief.

This was her home and life, for the moment, and she longed for him to appreciate and accept it. When Lucy and Maya removed their shoes at the door before entering the house, Flynn and Joshua observantly took note and did the same.

Lucy saw Flynn's sweeping glance over the interior, scrupulously clean but simply furnished with cozy rattan chairs, a low timber table and cushions where they sat on the floor to eat. Carved wood panels hung on the walls; a glass bowl filled with smooth stones and seashells sat on a narrow side bench.

Lucy led them through to one of two small side rooms separate by curtains. "This is our utility room," she explained, removing two rolled up mattresses and linen from a small cupboard. "Maya and I sleep next door. When you're unpacked and settled, come through to the kitchen at the back. I'll be making dinner."

She clenched her hands in apprehension, concerned over their opinion of such humble accommodation, but she need not have worried.

Joshua's eyes sparkled. "This is just like camping."

His happy, innocent comment dissolved any unease. Maya lingered, fascinated by their guests, leaving Lucy to prepare their meal alone. Through the thin walls, as she chopped vegetables, she heard Joshua and Maya chatting and smiled with pleasure as she worked. Then she heard their voices outdoors and presumed their visitors were being given a guided tour of the garden.

"Dinner," she called out the back door later when the boiled rice and simmered curry chicken was ready.

Flynn helped carry all the dishes of food to the low table and they sat around cross-legged, eating and talking, a pleasant milder breeze wafting in around them as night set in. It wasn't long before two small sets of eyelids grew heavy, so they settled the children into their beds after a tepid bath in the small basic bathroom. The kids were lulled to sleep by a steady evening downpour, drumming on the roof.

Lucy returned to the kitchen and boiled water on the gas stove for washing up, letting their few dishes drain and dry. She brewed coffee for Flynn and a refreshing cup of lemon ginger tea for herself. He carried the cane chairs out onto the front porch, and they sat in the steamy evening warmth watching streams of water run off the edges of the roof, forming large puddles on the ground and mini rivers along the roadside.

"It's coming into the wet season, so we're rarely short of water. One pipe runs into a tank, just in case. It will be wonderful for my vegetable garden," Lucy murmured as she sipped her hot drink. "And the rain will stop eventually, as suddenly as it started."

They shared an easy grin, but Lucy still felt a small knot of tension in her stomach. "How's everything in Mundarra?"

"Fine," was his noncommittal reply.

"Oh, you'll have to do better than that." She laughed. "Women need details. How's my big sister, Essie?"

"Appreciating the postcards and letters you send."

"I'm relieved to hear it. Is she keeping well? I haven't heard from her in a few weeks." He nodded. "And Carole's e-mails are sounding happier." Flynn remained thoughtful and silent. "I'm sorry. I'm babbling on here, enjoying an adult conversation in English for a change and you're probably weary from traveling."

"Not at all. It's great to have some down time."

"I'm surprised you managed so much time off. What happened about that new deal you were negotiating while I was there?"

"It could have gone through but, in the end, I decided against it." Lucy's eyebrows raised in surprise, and she didn't utter a word. He grinned. "I can hear you thinking, *Hard to believe*. I know. I've decided to ease back a bit," was all he said.

"Flynn Pedersen smelling the roses," she teased. "I'm astonished but pleased to hear it."

"At a certain point in our lives, I'm sure we all come to a new realization." As he spoke, his eyes covered her with a long steady look.

"We certainly do," she agreed softly, thinking of something else entirely, certain that he was too.

"I think I can finally understand your attraction to this place. It's peaceful and . . . rustic."

"Yes. These people are so hospitable and warm. The whole place has a seductive charm. Though it wasn't immediately after the tsunami," she recalled pensively. "It was the biggest in a century. Within ten minutes, a quarter of a million people were killed by the waves, and half a million were left homeless. When I first arrived, the devastation was appalling. There was virtually nothing left."

"It must have been distressing."

Lucy shrugged. "You learn to cope and just get on with it. There was certainly plenty of work to keep everyone occupied. Emergency relief supplies were rushed in from all over the world. We set up tents and worked in shifts registering and tracing separated children. Parents searched the relief camps for them, and we helped reunite families where we could." She grew thoughtful, remembering. "For a long time afterward, children came every morning to play football and games. We provided crayons and coloring books as an outlet for stress. UNICEF's focus is on education, of course, so they constructed hundreds of schools to earthquake resistance standards." Lucy released a long sigh. "After three years, reconstruction is almost complete, and lives are getting back to normal."

"I must say, I was surprised to learn you were living out here. You used to be farther north, closer to Aceh, didn't you?"

Lucy nodded, impressed that he knew, because she had never personally told him. "I finished my employment contract and decided not to renew."

Flynn snapped a glance at her, his eyes loaded with questions that he immediately voiced. "Are you planning to live here?"

Lucy nodded. "Only while I finalize Maya's adoption. That's why I rented this cottage. I wanted to create a more normal home life for her, but I plan to return to Australia to live and raise her."

At her disclosure, he just sat and gaped, stupidly grinning. Embarrassed by his attention and thrilled that he was pleased by her news, Lucy continued, "I do have some doubts about removing Maya from her native culture, but I'll always make sure it's part of her upbringing, and we'll make trips back here as she grows up."

Because Flynn had telegraphed the unspoken signal that he was glad about her eventual return to Australia, Lucy felt comfortable admitting, "I'm so glad you came."

"I told you. We both wanted to see you again. The main reason was to see you again." He hedged. "But when you were in Mundarra, you criticized me for what you believed was my undue focus on making money." Lucy felt embarrassed to remember. "I thought about it and, although I admit I was driven, that was never my only reason. Quite simply, I love a challenge but, more than that, as I told you, because I failed in marriage I felt, perhaps wrongly, that I needed to make up for it by being a good provider. You helped me realize that not everyone lives in such peace and comfort. So I asked Josh about spending the holidays up here. Let him compare his life to others and see how fortunate we are."

Lucy's heart swelled with deep love and respect for this man. "He's been watching everything closely. I'm sure he understands already."

So Lucy and Flynn formulated a schedule, one day at home and each alternate day found the four of them out sightseeing nearby in the region.

On home days they lazed and played simple games. Flynn and Joshua helped Lucy potter in the garden, and she cooked traditional Indonesian meals. Huge bowls of noodles and vegetable soup, beef curries, or nasi goreng and other rice dishes. And lots of fish.

The children usually picked the herbs and vegetables, Maya patiently teaching Joshua in her faltering but understandable English with many corrections and laughing in their communications. Maya clearly adored her pale-skinned new friend, "Yosh." Both Flynn and Lucy noticed his brotherly instinct to protect his softly spoken little guide.

Lucy and Flynn—spending time together in completely neutral and different surroundings—relaxed and delighted in each other's company. She learned to accept Flynn's offers of help with small maintenance jobs constantly needed about the cottage or heavier outdoor work, and found it an immense relief to share the burden. After years of living independently and being the one relied upon, she found it a huge liberation for someone else to make decisions and take responsibility. Flynn became her quiet strong shoulder of support, an element she'd never had in her life before.

Their awareness of each other grew stronger daily as emotional comfort changed to touches of more physical affection. A steadying hand at Lucy's elbow, quiet moments when he sought her hand and nothing else needed to be said, a warm hug or gentle smile in a mutual moment of joy. And every evening when the children were in bed, private time together to walk along the nearby unmade roads, talking, kissing, holding each other, freely allowing their love to grow.

Some days with the children they took a leisurely bicycle ride to nearby villages along roads lined with palms, fields of carrots, tomatoes, or cabbages, stopping at market stalls along the way. At one of them, Flynn bought Lucy and Maya each a seashell necklace, much to the girl's delight. She wore it constantly and refused to take it off. They always carried their clear plastic raincoats against sudden torrential downpours.

Other days, the four of them ventured farther afield using one of the local minivan bus services rattling along often inadequate roads through the countryside. They passed cocoa plantations, terraced rice paddies,

wooden pile houses on stilts with outside stairs leading
to upper balconies, always with the jungle-covered
hills and blue mountains a looming backdrop in the distance.

Joshua became their official group photographer,
catching them in happy spontaneous moments, record-
ing their discoveries along the way. His awe at the sight
of buffalo, deer, orangutans, or the simplicity and fragrant beauty of a frangipani, was innocent and conta-
gious. His small gestures of thoughtfulness toward Maya
warmed Lucy's heart. As if she were a delicate Asian
flower needing to be protected, he always seemed to be
watching out for her in a special way.

On one typically sultry evening, Flynn and Lucy
strolled near the house after the children were in bed,
exhausted after another busy day. It was not long before
Flynn and Joshua's imminent departure, and their murmured conversation turned reluctantly to Australia and
their return.

Flynn linked their fingers and said, "You mentioned
returning to Australia after Maya's adoption."

Lucy nodded, and they fell silent again. They ambled
a few steps farther before he halted and turned to face
her. "Do you have any idea where?"

Indulging in all the senses that drifted across a warm
Indonesian night with the man she adored, her mind relaxed and Lucy had to pull herself back to reality to answer his question. She let her mouth twitch into a grin
and looked around her. "As you can see, I love small
country towns."

"Would it be anywhere near Mundarra?"

She decided to skip any pretence. "Awfully close." He

smiled smugly as she explained, "Wherever Maya and I can find a place to live, really. I have something in mind. I've seen it already. A big house on the edge of town." She had no doubt her unsubtle hint would be understood. She couldn't have made it plainer if she'd held up a sign, and Lucy inhaled a breath of anticipation.

He stopped and kissed her on the nose. "I think I know the one you mean. It has plenty of rooms."

"In the guest wing maybe?" she teased.

"That's the other end of the house." He sounded appalled, dragging her closer. "I would hate to think of us living so far apart."

"Of course, I would pay rent."

He paused in their banter and said softly, "Wives don't pay rent."

Lucy stilled and whispered, "Are you proposing?"

"If you don't accept," he murmured, "I'll kidnap you and take you back anyway."

"No need to go to all that fuss." She wrinkled her nose. "I think I can safely say yes and mean it."

They shared another long passionate kiss, letting the dull sounds of night murmur around them, after which Flynn sighed. "I love you so much, Lucinda Greenwood Wilson."

"I love you too. Has quite a ring to it, doesn't it? My line of names."

"Speaking of rings. Let's all go shopping for one tomorrow so after Josh and I leave, you'll know it wasn't all a dream and no other man can snap you up while we're apart."

"We have to tell the children."

"First thing in the morning. If we tell them now and they're as excited as us, they'll never sleep."

Despite her happiness, Lucy paused. "Can I ask you something?"

"Anything."

"Why did you let me leave Australia two months ago without telling me how you felt? I got your text message, but it was hardly enough."

They had reached the house, so Flynn drew Lucy down beside him on the porch step. "I didn't come to the bus the morning you left because I didn't want to cause you any more distress. You'd been through so much after George died. I wanted to see you more emotionally settled. You had to return to Maya anyway. We both sensed an attraction but denied it. I didn't ask you to marry me then for two reasons.

"Firstly, I didn't want to tie you down and take you away from the work you loved. I wanted you to be absolutely sure this time and have no doubts. And secondly," he admitted, "because I'd failed in marriage once before, remember? For all the wrong reasons and on the rebound from losing you. But, I understand," he squeezed her hand to stem her apology. "I know you had things to do back then. I respect that now. We didn't mean to hurt one another, but it made me cautious. You've always been the one, but I didn't want to hurt you so I stepped back for a while to give our lives a chance to resolve themselves and find the right time to reconnect. I wanted to make sure this time we were both in the same place in our lives and both wanted the same thing."

"We sure do. We're going to be quite a blended family."

"Family," Flynn murmured. "I like the sound of that."

When Lucy and Flynn told Joshua of their engagement the next morning and their plans to marry as soon as she returned to Australia, he was ecstatic. It proved a little more difficult trying to explain to Maya that Joshua would be her brother and that she and her mother would be going for a long ride on a big plane one day soon. However, she caught their happy mood, and it was an excited foursome who piled into a local bus bound for Medan.

In a small jewelry shop, the selection process was swiftly achieved and consensus reached. Because the children thought it the prettiest and Lucy agreed, Flynn bought a coral-and-gold ring for his fiancée, a reminder of where he had proposed and the Indonesian connections they would always share. Once outside the shop, he lovingly slid it onto her finger, sealing the action with a kiss.

Two days later, it was time for Flynn and Joshua to leave, potentially sad but done quickly with whispered promises, hugs all around, and smiling anticipation of what was to come.

When Maya's bottom lip trembled, Lucy reassured her with a cuddle. "We'll see them soon. We're counting sleeps, remember?" She doggedly struggled against tears of her own as the mini bus rattled away.

With Flynn's connections, Maya's adoption proceedings were fast-tracked within weeks, not months, so Lucy and her daughter were soon on an international flight leaving Sumatra for the foreseeable future and heading south toward their new life and family in Australia.

One month later, in late summer, Lucinda Grace Greenwood Wilson walked slowly down the brick pathway lined with their few close family and friends in her half-sister's recently and completely renovated garden. She moved beneath an arched tunnel of beautifully fragrant climbing roses toward her future husband.

The simple ivory and lace gown fitted her slender body, and flowers had been tucked randomly into her long dark hair. Maya scattered rose petals before her as she approached Flynn, immaculate and handsome in a charcoal pinstriped suit, his face beaming with love.

Lucy briefly glanced around before she reached him and the marriage celebrant waiting for her beneath the filtered shade of an ancient gum tree. They were all there. Everyone who mattered to them. Anna and Karl Pedersen, Flynn's siblings, and their families. Essie, of course, her soft-gray eyes watery with happy tears. Carole and Roger with Amy and Ben. And Joshua, with great pain and negotiation temporarily released from his mother's custody for the special landmark event in his father's life.

More momentous, negotiations were underway and documents flying between Melbourne and Perth to grant Flynn permanent custody of his son, which Sandy was apparently prepared to consider for an additional financial consideration.

Now Lucy flashed Flynn a radiant contented smile as she reached his side and he whispered, "Hi."

The ceremony was brief, its words filled with meaning for the bridal couple. A casual celebratory meal was laid out in Roseleigh's magnificent dining room, spring cleaned and gleaming, every pedestal and sideboard brimming with scented bowls of pink and cream roses from the garden.

It was almost midnight before the bride and groom were finally alone, Joshua and Maya safely billeted with Carole's family for the week.

Flynn and Lucy sipped champagne and somehow also managed to shuffle about, dancing on the pool terrace of their lovely grand house on the outskirts of town to music drifting out to them from indoors, beneath an ebony velvet sky glittering with stars.

"It took twelve years, but we finally made it," Lucy grinned.

"It was worth the wait."

"Great idea of yours to stay here alone. So much has happened in recent months, it's a relief just to stay put."

They shared a secret smile and clinked glasses.

"Here's to us and our love," Flynn said.

"Amen to that. And our children. Present and future," she hinted.

Flynn chuckled. "Sounds promising. To our family and all it may hold."

"Oh, it's going to be wonderful," Lucy sighed, snuggling her head into her husband's shoulder.